LIGHTNING SCARRED AND OTHER STORIES

CAROLYN IVY STEIN

© 2021 Jeweled Sea Press

Carolyn Ivy Stein
Lightning Scarred and Other Stories

Published by: Jeweled Sea Press

Text Design by: Carolyn Ivy Stein

Original Art by: Anthony Cournoyer, Carolyn Ivy Stein

Stock Art by: @Melkor3D/Adobe Stock, @Marina/Adobe Stock, bourbonbourbon/Adobe Stock, @AnnstasAg/Adobe Stock, @falconnadix/Adobe Stock, @kuco/Adobe Stock, @Nejron Photo/Adobe Stock, @Olena/Adobe Stock

A CIP record for this book is available from the Library of Congress Cataloging-in-Publication Data

ISBN-10: 1-7370187-0-4

ISBN-13: 978-1-7370187-0-4

Carolyn Ivy Stein

Lightning Scarred and Other Stories

Jeweled Sea Press

Contents

ABOUT THE STORIES

In the 4th century BC, Pythias of Massalia became the first European to describe the far north. He coined the term "curdled water" to describe the ice-choked seas. He gave the name Thule to what he discovered there. Of course the Norse and Inuit knew of it long before Pythias.

I never intended to write about Vikings, but one day we were asked for proposals for microsettings to be used as stretch goals for a new game supplement, The Micronomicon by John D. Payne. We wrote about an Arctic portal that leads ships to a mystical land of ancient magic. We lightly tied it to Norse myth. After that, I knew that I wanted to write at least one story set there.

The first story set in Thule, "Lightning Scarred," was written as an inducement to get support for the game supplement and I thought we were done after that. But Thule wasn't done with me. Soon, Magnihild pushed into my writing again demanding new adventures, so I wrote "Lightning and Shadow." With just a map, a sledge, and a week's worth of food, Magnihild and Caedmon brave snow and ice on a mission to Thule, a brutal land of ice and magic. Will they survive the monsters and mages of the frozen waste?

After that, Thule beckoned me through her portal again and again, even when Vikings were the furthest thing from my mind. I added stories and eddas, folk tales in the Norse style that explore other aspects of Thulish gods and life.

"Frozen Art," is a loosely imagined fantasy based on one of my ancestors who traveled in a theater troupe across Europe, escaping pogroms and sailed a whaling ship with her family to Canada. But how did she get to New York City? I've imagined it this way. With little money and no connections, Raisa needed a Shabbat miracle to get to New York City. When she overheard an artist refusing to accompany an exploration ship to the Arctic, she knew the Queen of Shabbat brought magic to the far north just for her.

Once I realized that I didn't have to stick to Magnihild's viewpoint, I had more room to stretch. I wrote "Deep Compassion" about Yrsa who faces every mom's problem -- get a bunch of rambunctious kids fed and on their way to school in the morning. But for Yrsa, a sentient polar bear living in frozen Thule, morning means the first day of Arctic spring that ends her hibernation. Breakfast? Last summer's frozen seal meat. School transportation? A long hungry trek to a snowy shore with an ever-present chance of failure. So much hunger! But she won't eat just anything or anyone. Will her ethics get in the way of her survival and that of her cubs?

With "The Ginger Gambit" it is winter in the north and not a time for ships or Thule's magic. Magnihild's ginger cat has his own ideas on proper activities.

The last story in the collection was my most ambitious. I realized that I needed help, that the subject matter, Viking naval tactics, was too far outside of my comfort zone. Fortunately for the story, Steve is a naval military historian and he jumped onboard to help draft it. "Escape Into Winter" was written by both of us.

At the end of the book you'll find something written by someone other than me. A Viking professor arrived at my home waving a sheaf of papers, demanding that I publish his essay on his novel theory of magic and Thule. Strap in, it's a wild ride.

Thanks for picking up this book. I hope you enjoy reading the stories and eddas as much as I enjoyed writing them.

Be well, friends!

Carolyn Ivy Stein

THULE DISCOVERIES

Lightning
Scarred

CAROLYN IVY STEIN

Magnihild's long, thick brown braid hung down her back, swinging gently over her red wool cloak trimmed in white fox fur as the ship moved along the Barents Sea, taking her north to her betrothed. The rough sea jostled the ship, causing the large red and white striped square sail to thwap in time with the wind. Magnihild moved toward the bow to get a better look at their heading. That was a mistake. The wind blasted salty water droplets into Magnihild's mouth and eyes forcing her to blink rapidly to keep the burning salt from her delicate membranes.

A large wave crested under the ship. Magnihild clutched the smooth wooden rail to keep from being swept from her feet. One of her father's men laughed at her, but she ignored him.

It was Magnihild's last day of freedom. Tomorrow, as a freshly married wife, she would have to stay home to guard hearth and home instead of riding along with her father on sorties against the barbarians. That damned old sword!

This was not the worst of it. The worst was her father had decreed that she had to marry Caedmon. She acknowledged to herself that Caedmon was a strong, attractive man if one overlooked the plain evidence of his unfitness for any Jarl's daughter. He was a warrior so unlucky and so hated by the gods that he'd been struck by lightning. And lived. Thor marked him with lacy red scars covering his face, chest, and hands, inscribing him with lightning, making him unfit to enter any sacred place.

Some said it was a sign of the gods' favor that he'd lived at all. Magnihild didn't see a reason to choose between theories. It was obvious that he'd angered some gods and pleased others and they'd gone to war using his body as a proxy. Once his body and soul were joined to her own, she would take an equal part of all his enemies and allies. She didn't want a god as her enemy. She wasn't even sure she wanted a god as an ally.

"Magnihild, come help set up the tent," said Kolbyr, moving his aging, bulky form with the grace of the master swordsman and sailor he was. He'd been the first of Magnihild's father's vassals to swear his loyalty and was the only one of her father's men who dared tell her what to do.

"Let me be, Kolbyr. I am on watch."

He looked like he was about to scold her for her obvious lie, but then shrugged and ordered Royd, the youngest sailor on the cruise other than Magnihild herself, to help with the tent.

It was a bad sign that he gave up that easily, she thought. Kolbyr must think that she was no longer a warrior or a sailor, but just a woman on her way to her marriage who must be protected. She ground her teeth in frustration but resumed searching the horizon and the sea.

The days were getting shorter and Magnihild feared the darkness that would soon engulf them. Who knew what lay beneath the sea when the sky was lit only with moonlight, when they must depend on the gods' good favor to carry them safely across. Thankfully it would be at least an hour until the sun set tonight.

Their destination lay deep into Thule, the land of frozen wastes, monsters, and evil magic. Night there lasted longer than anywhere else in the known world. Sometimes for weeks. Sunless days rested heavy on Magnihild's soul, making her sick and sullen. Her mother said she was a creature of light.

She'd been trained to battle the lazy, settled barbarians along the Southern coasts where her father raided each spring, and she was good at it. She handled a sword as well as most of his men. She'd learned tactics and strategy from her father. She just wasn't sure how to prepare for battles with gods, especially when she didn't even know exactly which gods were upset with Caedmon.

Just to be safe she'd asked her father for animals to sacrifice to each of the gods before they left and to fund the celebrations to accompany each sacrifice. Her father agreed that it was the prudent course of action but said that resources were limited. He asked Magnihild to pick just one of the gods. She picked Jörd, mother of Thor the Thunderer, and goddess of the Earth. If any of the holy ones could help her, it was Jörd.

The ritual went well. Her father offered the very best goat to Jörd and her mother's servants prepared a feast no one would ever forget: rich pork stew, rye flatbread stuffed with honey and thyme and every kind of fish imaginable. For her part, she made a deep and sincere prayer to Jörd asking for Caedmon to be made worthy of her and her family.

In the middle of the circle dance, just after everyone finished eating her mother's pork stew and before the sweets to come, an ancient tarnished bronze sword fell from the wall, striking a glancing blow to Kolbyr, her father's oldest and most loyal sworn man. It knocked him unconscious.

Kolbyr recovered quickly but her father took it as a sign from Jörd. He ordered his round ship prepared and they left that evening bound for Thule to return the ancient sword to whatever god or demon wanted it.

Her father claimed that it was better to navigate at night because a seaman could take a reckoning from the stars, placed by Odin to help travelers. But she found the night eerie, filled with the promise of monsters and all manner of evils. As well, the night grew cold, making it more likely that the ship would hit ice in the water.

The wind picked up and soon her braid was bouncing around, smacking her face. The chill gale roughened her cheeks. She pulled her hood up over her head. The white fox trim warmed her skin and created a barrier to catch ice particles that swirled in the wind.

Ice magic was strange and eerie. Magnihild had heard about witches in Thule who had mastered the elements, who made fire erupt from ice. She'd heard of talking polar bears. She'd heard of snow-covered bushes twisted in strange shapes that suddenly shook their snow off revealing themselves as deformed women and giants.

The ship jolted over an ice chunk and Magnihild saw for a brief moment under the ice what looked like stone-hewn buildings arranged in a maze, a strange icy city that only gods or demons could inhabit. As she stared into the ice another wave crested over the ship soaking her and Royd as he tried to erect the sleeping tent out of the extra sail to protect their smelly sealskin sleeping bags and provide an extra layer of warmth while they slept in the bitter cold.

When the water cleared and she could see again, the city within the ice had disappeared. Ahead of the ship she saw ice had formed into an arch in the middle of the sea looking like a doorway into magic. A mist roiled within and around it, completely obscuring whatever lay beyond.

"Father, let us sail through the ice door," said Magnihild, struck by an idea. "Perhaps it will take us through to meet with the Aelfr. They could take this sword off your hands to return it to the gods. If we are polite to them."

Her father looked skeptical, the hard edges of his face assessing the ice as if it were an enemy stronghold, but when he turned back to Magnihild his eyes softened. "Through the ice, men. Let's make this a trip to remember."

As they angled the ship toward the enormous round hole in the ice, a gust caught the sail forcing the men to quickly adjust, using their strength against the wind. Magnihild wrapped sealskin sheets around the tarnished ancient sword in its red leather scabbard so that it would be safe as they moved through the mist.

"Row," called her father, and four stout fighters manned the oars to force the ship to turn and enter the hole in the ice, which shimmered in sapphire blue and royal purple, like melt lakes in the spring thaw. The mist surrounded the ship and Magnihild felt dizzy and overawed. This was a deeply unusual mist. Most mists were all the same, gray-white with indistinct objects. If she'd felt something in any of them it had just been wetness.

When the mist cleared the first thing she saw was a snow-covered land with more polar bears than she'd ever seen in one place. There must have been twenty or so wrestling, eating a seal, or rolling around on the snow. Hundreds of birds blackened the sky and called loudly, creating a cacophony in the air. It smelled of fresh fish and animals that gathered in the Arctic spring, as if the mist or the ice portal had led them from autumn to springtime.

Springtime meant...

Before she could complete her thought, three killer whales moved under the water, each one larger than their ship. The three moved their tails in unison, slapping the water with a crash to create an immense wave that crested above the ship. Icy water filled her mouth with salt, and she clung to the wooden rail with all her strength. How the ship stayed afloat under the force of it, Magnihild never knew. But the energy of the wave propelled the ship toward land where what looked like a small ship floated in the distance.

As they approached, Magnihild saw a knorr, a small merchant ship that carried settlers to new lands, marooned and sinking. The land nearby was mostly brown with streaks of dirt and low green plants and smelled of new life. Another sign of spring.

The knarr's passengers and crew: men, women, and children, had abandoned their ship and erected tents on the land near their wrecked ship. Around them were at least half a dozen vicious Arctic wolves, their white fur streaked with blood. She heard a child's high-pitched scream, though she couldn't see the child.

Her father ordered the men to row toward the beleaguered castaways. Those not rowing grabbed their weapons and prepared to fight.

Magnihild was irritated with herself that she hadn't brought her own sword. She pulled the ancient bronze sword from its seal skin wrapping and checked to make sure it drew easily from its scabbard, which she fastened to her belt. As the ship beached alongside the shore she and the men jumped out near the stern of the ship. The cold water came to her waist making her dress heavy and binding her legs as she ran to battle with her comrades against the wolves. As she charged, she drew the sword to keep it clear of the water.

"The sword! Look at the sword!" called one of her father's men.

Magnihild looked around dumbly searching for someone with a sword before she realized that he was pointing to her sword. The old, battered ancestral sword glowed with a pink light. In the brief time she took to quickly glance at it she saw that the tarnish was gone, and the sword shone in the light of the day. Or was the glow coming from within the sword itself? It felt heavier than before.

Magnihild roared her battle cry and rushed forward. To her left and right her father's men did the same. The clamoring commotion of their voices rising in righteous battle as they sped toward the encampment drew the wolves' attention from the unarmed settlers.

Thunder rumbled, as if the heavens also chose to join in this battle. The peculiar ozone smell of lightning filled the air as the sky flashed, reflecting in the ancient sword, which seemed to buzz against the palm of her hand with the power in the air.

As they came closer to the sight of the wolfish massacre, they saw men lying bleeding on the ground. Magnihild tried to ignore the sickening smell of blood and offal as she charged.

Their numbers and their loud voices stopped the wolves. They chased the majority of the large wolves away from the encampment and Magnihild thought they'd rescued the settlers when she heard a panicked shriek come from behind her.

Three large wolves had surrounded a lone elderly man carrying a small child. The man had a large stick that he was using like a sword to keep the wolves at bay, but Magnihild could see that it would be a matter of moments before the wolves defeated him.

The wolves circled closer.

Magnihild yelled her battle cry again and charged, hoping that the others would join her. It looked hopeless. Her voice rose in a rough entreaty, "Jörd, I have sacrificed to you. Bless us now! Help us, Jörd!"

Lightning drew a bright jagged line between her and the elderly man, illuminating the enormous wolf that had positioned himself behind the man. The wolf seized its moment and gracefully leaped at the man's back.

Time slowed and the wolf seemed to hang suspended in air for a moment.

Magnihild ran forward feeling blood beating in her ears. A veil of red fury came across her eyes and her mouth felt dry as she plunged her blade into the leaping wolf.

The elderly man pulled the child closer to his chest and ran toward the safety of their ship.

Magnihild was about to follow when a crashing boom engulfed her with a jolt of white, hot excruciating pain that seemed to originate from nowhere and everywhere. She felt herself surrounded by white. A purer white than snow and completely unlike like the soft gray mists.

The bright enduring white light seemed to come from both inside her and outside, preventing her from seeing anything else. A ringing in her ears nearly obscured all sound, though she could vaguely sense that men were shouting around her. She smelled pine resin and honey.

Her world went black.

When she regained consciousness, she found she was lying supine on the snowy plain surrounded by three enormous polar bears. She ached deep in her bones. Smoke rose from her chest where wool, linen, and skin had burned in the flash of a moment. She wanted to cry. She wanted to run. She wanted to move. But she couldn't do anything except listen.

A feminine voice boomed in the air, an imitation of the booming lightning that she'd felt in the... Minutes? Days? Years? that she'd been in the midst of battle with lightning dancing around her as she tried to save the man and the child.

"Take her back through," the voice said. "She will not live here for long, but in your own land, she has a chance of recovering. We shall keep her sword as our payment."

An enormous polar bear dominated her field of vision and stared down at her. Then the light flickered and Magnihild saw a majestic woman, a giantess, standing over her.

"Jörd!" Kolbyr gasped, sounding as if he were very far away.

She and the goddess were alone in a bubble of white. The beautiful face with deep blue eyes, white hair, and skin the color of pine bark smiled. She wore a white hood and cloak made entirely from polar bear fur and a brown sealskin dress that skimmed her enormous hips and shimmered in the white light. She smelled like pine trees, fresh fallen snow, and honey. She looked like nothing the earth could produce, for all that Jörd was goddess of the earth. Her majestic attention filled Magnihild with a quaking fear.

People beg the gods to smile upon them. But if they ever experienced it, they never would again. Jörd's smile was warm, yes, but the kind of warmth that melted everything it came into contact with, erasing all things we build, whether of snow or stone, and reformulating human beings into tools and weapons to serve the gods.

Finally, Jörd spoke to Magnihild in a deep feminine voice that held all the joy and terror of the world within it. "You are a worthy bride for Caedmon, our lightning-tested hero. We doubted you, but you did not hesitate to run heedlessly at enemies to save strangers. You are bold and audacious. You bear our marks, now and forever."

The giantess knelt down and stroked along Magnihild's cheek, causing an avalanche of pain to cascade through her body. Magnihild curled into herself, sobbing as the goddess touched her forehead and then along her right harm. When it seemed as if the pain would overcome her, the giantess rose and became a large furry polar bear again, which was honestly a relief. Mortals couldn't look upon the true forms of gods without changing or dying. Magnihild felt she was doing both, having seen Jörd's true form.

Her father lifted Magnihild into his arms, cuddling his god-damaged, lightning-scarred daughter. "You were brave," he whispered, but though he spoke to her, his eyes never left the Goddess' eyes.

"Hurry," said the polar bear. "You do not have much time. The gateway to your world will seal and will not unseal until the day the sun stands still in the sky. You must leave now and go through the faerie ring that brought you here or you will never see your loved ones again."

What faerie ring?

"The ice ring," her father said in a tone of revelation as if he had heard and was answering Magnihild's question. Kolbyr nodded agreement.

"Go! She has a wedding to attend."

"Wait." Magnihild pulled all of her strength into that one word. She reached for the polar bear. The goddess stopped, turning to Magnihild. In her enormous bear form she was both frightening and adorably furry. At least it didn't hurt to look upon her in this form.

Magnihild tried to muster the strength to ask her question. But couldn't.

The polar bear stared at her for a long moment, kindness in its white muzzle and dark eyes, before it responded to Magnihild's unspoken question.

"You are asking what happens next?" Jörd's voice boomed in her head but no one else reacted. They must not be able to hear Jörd speak, she thought.

Magnihild nodded. Even this small movement caused pain to jitter through her neck and she gasped.

"If you live through the next fortnight, you will wed our hero, Caedmon. When we call upon him, we will call upon you. Know that a time is coming when all life will be threatened. Polar ice will melt, and your people may perish if action is not taken. Courage will be required. Your lightning scars are my wedding gift to you to remind you of your courage. Treasure them."

The polar bear turned and swaggered up a hill of snow. Her movement seemed to be some sort of signal to the wolves that remained since they followed her as she moved further into the white continent.

The pack of wolves had killed all but seven of the castaways: the man and the child Magnihild saved, another two men, two small children, and a woman named Viveka who had hidden herself and the children in an ice cave and fought from that vantage point. Magnihild approved of the woman's fast thinking with wolves approaching from all sides. She'd make a good fighter.

Once everyone was on the ship, Magnihild noticed that Viveka was covered in gore. She wasn't sure whether the woman was injured or whether it was the blood of her companions, or whether it was wolf blood, but she asked her father to give Viveka one of her dresses to wear. The woman thanked her profusely.

Magnihild's own clothing had burned wherever the lightning struck, so that her best wool cloak and linen shift had several singed holes that smelled of burnt hair and, incongruously, of the sharp resin of pine trees and the sweet smell of honey. She wrapped the cloak more tightly around herself and refused Kolbyr's offer to bring her another dress. This dress and cloak had been touched by Jörd. Like the lightning burns decorating her body, they were sacred. Goddess-touched.

Kolbyr and her father spread out a sealskin sleeping bag and tried to put her inside, but Magnihild didn't want to miss seeing what could be seen in the land of Thule before they left. She asked Kolbyr to help her stand.

He levered her up to the railing and wrapped his arm around her back, providing just the smallest support to keep her from collapsing. Magnihild drank in the moment, recognizing in his manner the respect she'd earned as a warrior and as a woman. She didn't say anything, not wanting to embarrass either of them, but she leaned into his arm and smiled at him. He smiled back as if he were her own proud father.

The ship approached the melting ice portal and patchy sections of mist that did not entirely fill the hole floated within. Even as the ship approached the ice portal, Magnihild could see the mist dispersing and cracks appearing in the ice. They didn't have much time left.

"To oars," her father cried, and the men pushed the ship forward, trying to catch the mist before it vanished, trapping them in the Thule.

As the ship entered the portal, a hunk of melting ice cracked and broke off from the top of the portal, falling at Magnihild's feet. The boom of the ice block against the deck of the ship echoed in her ears and she thought she heard the word, "Remember." The mist engulfed the ship and Magnihild felt a familiar dizziness and a strange taste in her mouth.

As they pressed through the mist, pressure enveloped her head creating the worst headache she'd ever had. Strange greenish lights floated in wisps in the night sky and the weather changed from the warm spring day to bitter Arctic night.

They sailed through the night and Magnihild kept watch, though the slight pain in her head never ceased. She did not want to miss one moment of this voyage. When the ship finally arrived at Caedmon's home port, they learned that they had been gone for exactly a year, though it had felt like less than a day.

"It's the nature of Faerie lands to shift with time," said Kolbyr as if that settled everything. "Be grateful that you arrived here before he took another to wed.

Magnihild nodded but she secretly thought that Jörd had arranged it this way. If they were to be Jörd's wedded champions, she had to arrive at the proper time, which must be now.

EDDA - SIF'S YELLOW CLOAK

Translated from the Chronicle of Jörd; Author unknown

Jörd, daughter of Nott, moth-
er of Thor, summoned Loki.
"Tell me where Sif's yellow cloak has gone."
Loki's fire eyes glinted as he cocked his head.
"Mother of Earth, perhaps Thor's wife is as
man-mad as the beauteous Freyia."
"Never," said Jörd, her eyes glittering dangerously.
She cracked her knuckles sending earth-
ly weasels quivering to their dens.
The smell of burning fields rose from her hands.
"All the Æsir know you wound with evil jokes, Loki.
Slander faithful Sif again and I mix your
mead with malice and murder."

Loki grinned, his voice like a sword. "Sif
hides her cloak with her lover.
Or her lover hides inside her cloak."
Loki twisted his hands before Jörd
making the lover's sign.

Furious then was Jörd. She paced and snorted in rage.
Each pounding footfall caused the land
to tremble and split asunder.
Fish burst from water into air, flop-
ping down on the shore.
Maps of the shifting coasts turned as useless as a fouled sail on a sinking longship.

Loki laughed. "I am parched. My
throat is too sore to speak.
Bring your best mead. Then the
truth is yours for a price."

Jörd stopped pacing and swung around to
look at the trickster god. "What price?"

"A price so small, a giantess like
you will barely notice it."
Loki coughed and coughed again.
"But not another word
until good mead sluices over my dusty throat."

Jörd brought a giant carved-clay tank-
er, large as a stout man,
with honey-sweet mead spilling from the rim.

The thirsty god drained it entire in one large gulp.
He pressed the tankard to her for more.

"You're light-hearted, Loki, greed-
ily drinking my best mead.
Mocking my daughter-in-law's virtue. Speak now.
Show me Sif's fine yellow cloak."

"Fair Jörd," Loki said, his voice slid-
ing like seal fat over ice.
"Give me what is under the cloak as payment."

Jörd's cunning gaze transformed her massive face as greed filled her heart.
"Malevolent Loki, if you want what is hidden it is because you are trying to trick me.
But I am too cunning for you. If you want
it, then that is what I shall take.
Whatever Sif hides under her cloak
is mine. Pick another prize."

Loki argued, but Jörd was resolute.
Finally, Loki said, "Give me your ring and I
will show you what is under the cloak."

Jörd twisted the gold ring with its blood
dark gemstone and tossed it to Loki.
He placed it on his wrist, admir-
ing the fit of the massive ring.
Then he nodded and held out a hand.
"Come with me, Jörd, to see wonders hidden beneath Sif's yellow cloak."

Jörd placed his burning hand over her
icy one as he led her to Midgard.
They walked north and north again.
They came to a shimmering yellow curtain that hid its prize so well
even Jörd couldn't fathom the wonders within.

Loki said, "Do you still want what is hidden, fair Jörd?

She touched the curtain and it parted for her.
"It is mine, Loki. You will have none of it."
Jörd rushed forward ahead of Loki
to see her icy treasure.

With that, Loki stepped back through
the yellow curtain into Midgard,
He folded up the cloak and trapped Jörd
there, on the frigid shores of Thule.

The giantess roared. Whales fled.
Loki's crystal laugh fell like ice on her ears.

"In this icebound land, you shall sit from
morning to night, and night to morn.
Sif hid this place from you. Now her yellow cloak shall hide me from Thor.
The pretty Sif is a finer mead than that provided by you, Jörd, mother of Thor.
I will drink my fill."

Jörd's anguish echoed like seal song from ice to sea to land across all of Thule. Hush. Listen. You can hear her song carried by the North wind.

Ice Witch

Adventures

LIGHTNING AND SHADOW

CAROLYN IVY STEIN

Magnihild's boots squeaked as she stepped through the freshly fallen snow that blanketed the mountainside. The wind sliced like an icy dagger against her skin even through the woolen dress and cloak she wore. Her best festival mittens lined with soft white fox fur kept her hands warm at least, though they were too fancy for a trek through the wilderness and too special to risk staining or losing. But Caedmon had pointed out that it was always best to present one's best face when asking for a boon from dangerous creatures. Her festival gloves were the only item of clothing she had that was both beautiful and suitable to the elements.

Caedmon, also dressed in his warmest clothing, dragged a rawhide and wooden sledge packed tight with tørrfisk, hard rye bread, a change of clothing, and patties of fuel to melt ice to drink. It made a dull breakfast and Magnihild found herself wishing for her mother's porridge with bits of dried fruit. The sledge contained all they needed to survive on their own as well as a tightly wrapped parcel of trade goods to use in negotiations, if they found anyone to negotiate with. But it was a dull survival.

Safely ensconced in the bodice of Magnihild's dress was a sealskin map drawn by a member of one of the Inuit tribes. The tribe sold the map with the sunstone location to Magnihild's father for six iron axes and a bright blue wool cloak that had belonged to her mother before the plague spread through their home.

Neither of them knew what they would find in Thule's center, nor were the kingdom's elders or the Inuits who sold them the map much help. Some said that sunstones lay in heaps in the middle of the snow. Others, that a beautiful garden lay within the deepest center of the land, powered by sunstones scattered heedlessly about by Freyr. Some said that the sunstones were used in unholy worship ceremonies that no one could describe. Still others claimed that sunstones could only be had through clever deals with the ice witches. Magnihild knew Caedmon as a canny trader, so she hoped it was the last option.

Two things were certain: First, Caedmon and Magnihild were the only ones known to survive godly lightning and were the only ones who could get through alive. Second, without the magic held within the sunstone, the healer's spells would continue to fail, their people would continue to die. Every year there were fewer of them in town. Every year more children and elders died of simple diseases that the healers should have been able to cure. The power of the sunstones would reverse that trend.

The extra layer of soft snow made the sledge easier to pull even as it impeded Magnihild's own footsteps. Night came early here at this time of the year. As the sun set leaving the sky rippling with the colors of bruised skin, the increased cold prevented the sledge from moving easily. While they both wanted to find the witches and their rumored city of ice as soon as they could, it made no sense to expend energy pulling the sledge in poor conditions. Even taking breaks, alternating sledge-pulling duty, and stopping when the temperature dropped, they still couldn't eat enough for their bodies' needs.

Magnihild could see Caedmon's muscles standing out within his lightning-scarred skin since he'd lost the fat that covered them. She knew she must also be losing weight as they fought the cold and ice. His red-brown hair, normally so neatly combed and caught in a warrior braid, was stiff with seal fat and dusted with a light coating of snow. Even his beard was covered with a layer of little ice crystals formed by the snow.

Magnihild knew she must look similarly icy and disheveled, but she had ceased to care about her appearance the day she'd been struck by lightning. She bore the scars of that day all over her body in the form of red lines that looked like fine branches of trees. A year later she still felt random pains that moved along the branches of the lightning strikes and terrible headaches that sent her to bed for days at a time. No one but her husband Caedmon, who had undergone the same terrible test, understood how it felt.

She'd thought that had been the worst challenge she'd ever faced. But now the desperate tedium and hunger of the long days of walking and pulling the sledge without a single sign of gods, demons, gardens, or ice witches brought her to despair. With each step Magnihild felt more and more that this was a fool's errand.

Each step felt heavier than the last and she couldn't remember ever feeling truly warm. She knew that Caedmon must be feeling the same. After a year of marriage, she could read his moods by the slight downturn of his full lips, rough from the wind, and the movements of his hazel eyes.

They had packed their sledge with enough food, fuel, and clothing for a month-long journey. Or so they'd thought. Only two weeks had passed since they left their ship in the hands of Caedmon's captain and started alone on the trek to the ice witches. They only had enough food left for another week unless they got lucky and found something they could kill and eat. So far the route to the sunstones hadn't crossed any animal migration pathways. They'd seen a seal, but it had dived as soon as it spotted them. Caedmon had flung his axe, but he'd missed and now his axe lay somewhere under the ice at the bottom of the frozen sea.

Last night, wrapped in their sealskin sleeping bags, their legs entwined more for warmth than passion, she'd wondered if Caedmon would turn back if she pretended to be sick. She worked it out in her head, deciding on the exact sort of illness and when she would do it. She'd made the same strategic decisions every night for the last five nights of gloom and muscle pain. But as each day danwed, her pride would not let her give up as long as Caedmon depended on her.

Hadn't Jörd said that she would be a worthy fighter by her husband's side? What kind of fighter gave up in the face of an adversary? And what kind of adversary was snow? So, each day she found herself pulling the sledge in her turn, fighting against the pain caused by uncaring snow and muscle-testing mountains. It was easier to face a human enemy than the cold dispassionate environment.

Each morning she prayed. Jörd? Are you watching over us? Will you keep us safe? Please show us food. Protect us, Jörd.

Jörd never answered her silent prayer but she had met the goddess once and trusted the gods weren't done with her or Caedmon yet.

The sledge stopped.

Caedmon pulled, but it didn't budge.

"Wait, let me check," Magnihild said. She looked underneath for rough ice, but it seemed as smooth as ever. She pulled off one embroidered mitten and ran a finger along the cold runner. She felt clumps of ice underneath the wood. No wonder it had stopped. Mere wood wasn't slick enough to make a heavy sledge easy to pull.

"We need to re-coat the rails," she said.

Caedmon slumped and rubbed his face and eyes with his gloved hand, then shook his hand as if he were trying to get blood to flow back into it.

"Rest a bit," Magnihild said. "I'll take care of the runners." She took a deep breath, feeling the icy air chill her lungs, waking her and giving her a few more moments of strength. The air tasted of resin and ice.

She pulled out a leather bag with the glop they'd made of moss and slightly rancid seal fat and tipped the sledge onto its side. It shouldn't, but the greasy smell brought a rumble from her stomach. Ignoring it, she dipped a strip of polar bear hide into the bag and applied a layer to the runners. Then she swigged a mouthful of water and spit it along the rails. In this weather, it froze quickly, which was a blessing. She patiently applied three more layers of fat and water, scraping each until they presented a smooth surface that would allow the sledge to slip along the ice.

Once she was done, the rails had a slick surface that would glide along the ice until it was time to resurface the runners again. She thought it would be enough to keep them going until the end of the day. They were lucky that the ground was smooth today with solid ice and a heavy coating of snow. In worse terrain they would have had to stop and redo the coating several times in a day. Perhaps Jörd was looking out for them with that heavy snowfall, after all.

She smiled up at Caedmon. He was rubbing his left wrist vigorously.

"Lightning pain?" she asked.

"I don't think so. Probably just the weight of the sledge."

She pulled his hand toward her and slipped off his mitten. She thought she knew his hand as well as her own by now, but it looked different today. His pale skin was even paler. Was the cold causing damage? The lightning marks also looked strange, but she couldn't figure out the difference. The scars couldn't move, could they? She was sure the feathery pattern bent left, but it was bending right. Her earlier impression must have been mistaken. She guided his hand inside her cloak, warming the skin with her own body heat.

"Is it both hands or just the one?" she asked.

"Just the one."

She nodded. "Is the warmth helping?"

"Yes."

Unlikely to be lightning pain then. Nothing stopped that. Not warmth. Not ice. Nothing.

"I will take my turn pulling the sledge, while you rest your hand," she said.

"My turn isn't over. And I'm stronger than you are."

In truth he looked anything but strong as he hunched over, lines of weariness forming at the edges of his eyes and along his forehead.

"True enough. You will need to reserve your strength so that you can take over for me when I weaken. I'll be okay. You know it is always easiest when the runners are freshly coated," she said lightly.

He grunted.

Exhaustion painted every crease in his face. The lightning marks seemed a brighter red, though that was probably because his skin was paler. She wished that they could turn around and head home. Not just for her own sake, but for the man she'd grown to love in the last year. But if they did, they would be called cowards and people would die for today's short-lived comfort. She knew Caedmon would never agree to that. And, despite her own misgivings, she wouldn't want that either. Better to die trying to save one's kin than live in ignominy.

Magnihild handed the map to Caedmon to determine their route. She gripped the wooden bar across the top of the sled and dragged it forward. She'd gone only a few feet when the sledge stopped moving, jerking her back. She fell on her rear end into the snow.

"That shouldn't happen. The rails should be slick." Her voice had a whining tone that shamed her as she spoke. "We should be good for at least a few hours before we need to reapply the moss."

"Could be there's something under the snow. Help me dig, Magnihild," he said.

Together they moved aside several feet of light, powdery snow and uncovered a wall and ceiling of intricately carved ice deep under the snow. Inside, they could see a gently flickering light, as if a fire raged within. But no ice wall could stand up to fire. It had to be something else.

It took them an hour, but they finally moved enough snow to reveal a house made entirely from carved ice beneath the surface of the snow and ice. Abstract images of whales, octopuses, and seals adorned the door which had a small opening and a piece of hide hanging invitingly outside. Whatever was inside looked enormous and moved like liquid, appearing and disappearing beyond the translucent ice walls.

Her stomach roiled as if she had eaten the rancid seal fat and moss that coated the rails and her skin tingled all over as if a thousand small insects had taken up residence. She shook as she pressed her face against the cold ice wall. She hungered to see the large figure inside but felt a howling anger speaking into her mind, a hunger for freedom and destruction.

"Let's go inside," Caedmon said.

Magnihild was already pulling the piece of hide, pushing her body as close as possible to the icy walls, craving knowledge of the creature behind the door. From another dimension she could hear her sensible self tell her body to stop, to consider that there might be danger within.

She pulled again at the hanging hide, but it didn't open. She could see a glow of power, like a sunstone still buried under ice and snow. She tried to reach for it as she pulled at the strip of hide, but it slipped out of place and slid further into the snow. To make matters worse, the door still wouldn't open.

Why was everything stuck today? She could ask Caedmon to help her but she was impatient to see the shapes she felt moving within, so she ignored him and put her strength into one last pull.

"Stop."

She froze.

The voice was thin and reedy like the sound of wind whistling through trees, but it carried into the spaces in the far corner of her heart that even her sensible mind couldn't penetrate.

"Leave it be," the voice said.

Reluctantly, Magnihild dropped the piece of hide and turned toward the voice. She saw a woman dressed completely in white from the white fur hood to her white leather boots. Even her long braids were white tied with white leather ribbons. Ice witch?

The stranger muttered something to herself and made an almost casual hand motion. She twisted her wrist and a flurry of snow from her hand swirled around all three of them. As the snowstorm picked up speed, it dumped a coating of snow over the ice building they'd just unearthed. Hours of work wasted.

"Leave this place," the witch said.

"We cannot. We have business here," Caedmon said. Magnihild could tell by the way his eyes slid back to the carved ice door that he longed to get back to the work of entering it.

The witch shook her head. "You are unwelcome strangers. Depart while you can still do so under your own power. This part of the world is not made for you. You will find nothing here but death."

As if to illustrate her words, a large white beast leapt into their midst heading for the unarmed witch. The woman motioned in the air and the snowfall escalated into a blizzard that swirled like a cyclone. An ice wall appeared from nowhere and crashed to the ground, shards of ice flying through the air.

Magnihild reached for her sword but Caedmon was faster, his sword almost flew into his hand as he stepped between the woman and the enormous bear, for that was what had invaded their convocation. He brought his sword down with single powerful stroke over the great beast's head.

Magnihild lunged forward, plunging the sword into the beast's side. It would have been enough to kill an ordinary beast, but this bear was extraordinarily large and covered in thick fur that deflected their swords. The swords slid against the bear's fur, missing vital organs. The beast would die from the wounds, certainly, but not before it killed them.

Magnihild was the closest and the beast raked its claws across her dress, rending her cloak, ripping through her dress, and causing one of her dress brooches to fly across the snow. She felt pain burn down her left ribcage and the wet heat of her own blood as it soaked through her clothing.

The witch muttered something in a strange language. An ice spear slid from the center of the storm and flew as if launched by a bow. It embedded itself in the polar bear's fur. The great beast fell. His blood coated the white landscape as it poured from him, freezing in swirls of red on the ice. To Magnihild, hungry as she was, it smelled like food and she imagined cooking it.

Caedmon leveled his sword at the witch but Magnihild put her hand on his and gently pushed the sword down.

"I think we can parley with the witches. Can't we?" She gazed steadily at the ice witch as if she could force compliance through her eyes alone.

The ice witch, if that was indeed what she was, lifted her chin and the storm intensified around them. It lashed Magnihild's cheeks. She could barely see Caedmon next to her through the swirling snow.

"We are here to trade," Caedmon said raising his voice to shout into the whirlwind.

"We provide for ourselves, and we have no need for your iron tools or ugly fabrics. Begone!" The witch drew herself up and it seemed to Magnihild that she grew taller and broader.

The wind tugged at the cloak Magnihild had wrapped tightly over her head and it fell away from her face, exposing her cheeks to pelting ice crystals. The witch stepped forward and touched the lightning scars on Magnihild's cheek. Underneath the woman's fingers little sparks rose from her lightning scars, burning and tingling.

The witch nodded to herself and then turned to Caedmon, pulling his scarf from his face and fingering his lightning scarred cheeks. An involuntary moan escaped Caedmon's lips and Magnihild could see the lightning rising from the witch's fingers whenever she touched the scarring.

Apparently satisfied, the witch stepped back into the center of the storm and raised her arms to the sky. The swirling curtain of snow congealed into shapes all around them but they hovered just beyond Magnihild's gaze. She wasn't sure what she was seeing. Then one of the shapes closest to the witch, a large twisted thing about the height of her father's largest warrior and the width of two of him put together shook itself and the snow fell off.

The immense figure walked to the side of the ice witch and Magnihild realized it was the largest woman Magnihild had ever seen. Looking into the strange blue eyes and cheeks tattooed with the symbol of Thor, Magnihild thought that it was some sort of non-human, a giantess perhaps. The giantess patted the witch, who bent her head respectfully. Then the giantess closed the distance between Magnihild and Caedmon.

Part of Magnihild felt giddy to be in the presences of such power, part of her quavered in fear. The trained Viking warrior within her made note of six ways she could escape or turn the situation to a victory if the giantess attacked.

"Are you here for food, children?" the giantess asked. Her voice sounded as cold as the wind whipping the waves during a storm but did not seem unkind for all that. "You may take this polar bear with you as our gift to succor you as you return to the sea. This is in recognition of your bravery against the mad Kaneedma. It shall keep you fed long enough to rejoin your companions."

"No, Honored One. We have come to find sunstones. We can pay a good price for them, but we cannot leave without what we came for," said Caedmon. His voice deepened to the one he used in court when he spoke as his father's representative.

Magnihild wasn't sure it was wise to be so direct with what they needed, but her only experience with merchants was raiding them with her father. In that activity, speed and misdirection were key and excessive talking was simply unwise. But trade was Caedmon's expertise and they'd agreed that he'd handle it if they found witches or others who might have sunstones.

"As you can see, we lack for nothing." The witch waved her hand in the air pointing behind her. "We do not need you or your possessions. Our sunstones are not for sale."

So, they did have sunstones. Good. If the negotiations did not go well, they could always conduct a night raid and take them.

The swirling snow settled on round buildings and towers formed from ice blocks reaching three stories high. Lights flickered within some of the buildings and ice witches of all sizes, from as large as a double-sized man to as small as an arctic hare, moved through the packed snow streets. Magnihild swore the city had not been there before. They couldn't have missed an entire city, could they have? She blinked, feeling the ice crystals along her lashes graze and then melt against her cheeks.

"Nonetheless, I am Caedmon. This is Magnihild, my wife and true companion. We journeyed from beyond the Great Northern Sea to speak with you and to trade. We request your hospitality."

Magnihild gasped. Asking for hospitality meant putting their lives and safety at the hands of these frightening women. Who knew if they even understood the duty of a host out here in the northern wasteland? She had heard of travelers who ventured far to the south in the Mediterranean Sea relying on hospitality who had been robbed or killed.

Worse still, it bound Magnihild and Caedmon, tying their hands. It meant that they couldn't simply conduct a raid for the sunstones and be on their way. This complicated matters. Not for the first time, Magnihild appreciated her father's wisdom in keeping to their own kind and raiding for what they couldn't supply on their own.

On the other hand, looking around at the mysterious city that had appeared before their eyes, raiding the ice witches might not be wise. Knowing who not to raid was as much a part of strategy and tactics as knowing how to form men into integrated raiding parties. Perhaps her husband was right to give up this option in favor of the hospitality that would bind both parties.

She looked around the city. The buildings looked as if they had been carved from diamonds. She smelled a delicious stew and salivated. She was so hungry. Even if the witches extended hospitality toward them, she doubted that they would share their food. In truth, she doubted that anyone living so far from the civilized world knew what hospitality was.

"We pledge hospitality to you. But we are not interested in trading our sunstones. It is difficult even for us to find more," the giantess said gently. "We will give you a place to sleep tonight and a meal, then you must go back to your home."

Caedmon unstrapped the load from the sledge and reached for the box with the salt, spices, gems, and amber that they'd brought to trade. They'd packed most valuable trade goods that their two kingdoms could afford. "We can pay for sunstones. Please just take a look and consider—"

A crack of thunder echoed through the icy city and shook the ground. At the same time a surge of agony radiated along Magnihild's spine scalding her skin. Her vision blurred. An intense pressure slammed into her brain. She cried out and tried desperately to stay upright but she tottered and nearly fell. In her personal crimson cave of pain, thoughts took a long time to resolve.

Lightning pain. The worst yet.

As it cleared, she saw Caedmon sprawled on the ground, convulsing. The giantess stepped past them and at first

Magnihild thought the witches were attacking them but quickly realized they were running toward something else. Two witches were flung into the air by an unseen force and landed hard near Caedmon. Since they were witches, perhaps they could survive, but nothing human would have survived that.

She struggled to stand and gawked. Someone—no something had broken free of the carved ice house under the snow. All of the witches converged and skirmished with their spells but they didn't affect the beast.

Nothing should have been able to remain in shadow against the blinding white snow, but whatever had escaped seemed to be indistinct, as if it were creeping through the world in halfway slices, transforming as it moved. One moment it was a tentacled monster, the next it was a cloud of fog. One moment it resembled a man. The next it was a killer whale beached on the icy shore. It rippled through forms, indistinct, appearing as through it were engulfed in swells of sea water.

Magnihild gagged on the miasma of rotten fish and dead seals that rose from the ice house as she struggled to join the fight.

A voice spoke in her head. "This is anti-life. It must be destroyed or contained."

Was it her own thought? The witches? Jörd?

"Where is the sunstone?"

Magnihild wasn't sure who had shouted, perhaps one of the witches. Magnihild gripped her sword. From the corner of her eye she saw Caedmon rise with his sword. He looked terrible, but he breathed in the icy air and ran toward their foe. Magnihild followed.

"Stop." The witch they had first encountered seized Magnihild's arm causing her to stagger back. "Lightning. There is a better way." She reached into her sleeve and pulled out the largest sunstone Magnihild had ever seen and pressed it against Magnihild's chest. There was intense agony, but this time Magnihild remained upright. She heard the same voice in her head.

"Lightning can still the anti-life. Do it."

In that moment, Magnihild saw what she had to do. She raised her arms as the witch pressed the sunstone against her heart. The power buzzed within her, burning her skin. Water froze on her face. The only relief from the pain came from her own tears.

She cried out as another wave of pain crashed through her. This time the very air crackled and exploded into sharp, colored light.

"Again," said the voice within her.

The sunstone's power seared the lines of her lightning scars again and again until lightning erupted from her upturned hands.

This time the witches were prepared for it and they caught the lightning in a cage of ice, wrapping it around the indistinct form of the beast. As she watched, they lowered the caged beast into the ice house, her lightning stabilizing their icy magic.

They must have trapped it. They must have covered the house with piles of snow. They must have taken Magnihild into their city, because when she woke up she was in a proper bed with shafts of sunlight creating rainbows through the ice walls. Caedmon slept nearby, his snoring familiar and comforting. The rich smell of stew permeated the air; she could almost taste it. She could have eaten the polar bear all by herself, no cooking required. She was that hungry.

When the witches finally sent her and Caedmon home, it was with the sunstone used to activate her lightning. It was a gift, they said. Caedmon insisted that they accept a reciprocal gift of spices and the gems, which they did. They also left with the polar bear neatly butchered and stored on the sledge. With that and the remaining tørrfisk and dried rye bread, they had enough food to get them to their ship and home, as well.

The witches also gave her a functional pair of white gloves. Her embroidered red festival gloves had burned up from the lightning that streamed from her hands. She shouldn't care about their loss, it was a small price to pay for a sunstone that would allow their healer to save their people, but she missed them, nonetheless. She would make a new pair, she decided, but instead of embroidering flowers she'd make this pair white in honor of the witches with embroidered lightning bolts.

It seemed only right and proper.

EDDA - BIRTH OF THE ICE WITCHES
Fragment from the Drang Isle Edda; Author unknown

Hungry for companionship, Jörd created a castle of snow and beckoned the white bears to join her.

Cozy in her winter palace with the dumb beasts, she bore and raised many wise bears as sons and daughters. The Kaneedma, this race of ice bears born fully furred but imbued with the giantess' cunning, were her most loyal friends and followers in Thule. She spent long hours with her wise friends playing games and eating seals.

One day, a ship lost its way through the ice portal into the land of Thule. At first the sailors were terrified by the Kaneedma's jaws and man-like ways. But Jörd bade them welcome, so desirous was she for new faces in Thule. The sailors enjoyed Jörd's mead and meat. They slept the nights in her icy palace until the solstice came once more and they sailed home again.

From these men, the giantess bore many daughters, all tall, shapely women with white skin and silver hair. From them sprang the race of ice witches who even now guard Thule's land from monsters and men.

The saying runs thus: In the age of the blood-soaked moon, a woman born of ice witch and half-breed god shall crack open Thule's shell and release the night. Then man and beast will die in waves of blood hot seas and bitter regret.

OLD AND NEW

FROZEN ART

CAROLYN IVY STEIN

Raisa hadn't thought herself capable of missing Shabbat in Botosani. She shivered in the bitter cold of spring in Nova Scotia and wished she were sitting on sweet green grass with her feet in the blue-brown water of the Dresleuca River, wavelets lapping against her feet until they wrinkled like raisins in the sun.

In Botosani, she'd be helping her mother prepare for Shabbat, welcoming Friday night as if it were a bride or a queen, deserving of the finest linens and candlesticks. They'd serve the best bread and wine they could. She'd comb her long wavy black hair and rub rose-scented oil into it until it shone like a mirror framing her pale face, ready for the peace and grace of Shabbat.

There would be none of that tonight.

Raisa worked her knife in another fish, tossed yet another stinking pile of fish guts into the barrel, hearing it slap wetly against the other contents. The rest of the fish went into another barrel, which would eventually be salted and dried in the sun. She wished she hadn't left. It snowed in Romania too, but not like the frozen wastes of this strange country.

She repeated the country name to herself again: Canada. They spoke French and English. Her French was improving slowly, but she needed to learn faster if she wanted a better job or even survive once they managed to get to Quebec. It was hard enough to do here where a dozen different languages could be heard in the salt fish factory.

Her father kept encouraging her to learn English, claiming they would soon go to New York, where many other Botosani Jews had settled.

Her mother said that Raisa needed a husband, not another job, but it wasn't true, and they all knew it. The family needed money to buy passage on another ship to Quebec or to Philadelphia or to Daddy's mysterious New York City. So, Raisa gutted fish through the day while her mother worked at a laundry for sailors.

Her father hadn't yet found steady work. There was little need for fine tailors, and even less need for singers or actors in a land of ice, seals, and gentiles. Still, he tried.

Raisa knew that he sang on the town's main street waiting for the occasional coin drop into his hat. He did piece work repairing clothing or sails, whatever the townsmen brought him while he sat in the laundry with her mother. But what worked in Prague and Berlin didn't work as well in the frozen land they found themselves in. For one thing, the harsh air dried his throat something fierce. For another, money seemed scarce among the fish workers. Work from sailors ebbed and flowed, much as the sea itself did.

Tonight, Friday night, was Shabbat, and there was no challah or suitable wine to be found anywhere. Still she looked forward to it, for the peace of the day if nothing else.

She finished her shift at the cannery, and pulled her coat and shawl over her shivering arms and head. Some of the other girls kept their coats on while they worked, but Raisa couldn't bear the smell and didn't want it to permeate her best coat. Her only coat, she corrected herself silently and with some irritation.

She'd protected her special items for months as her family had walked across Europe and England, performing along the way, until they reached Liverpool. They bartered for passage on a whaling vessel, and she sold the lovely crimson coat with the ermine collar and her wedding dress to help with the money for the passage. She didn't miss the wedding dress; it had never been worn.

She longed for the beautiful coat that had kept her so warm during their travels. When they had disembarked from the ship she looked like a ragamuffin dressed in her worst clothing, now her only clothing. They had nothing left to sell, even if there had been a place to sell it in this wretched town.

She walked down the snowy street, listening the squeaking of her shoes on the packed snow, slipping a bit on the ice as she made her way to the laundry where her mother worked.

The one precious item she had refused to sell to the greedy merchants was her pack of paints, pencils, and paper. Each evening she sat and drew as she awaited her mother, feeling the quiet and calm of the evening settle over her. The laundry smelled like warmth and fragrant soap, a balm to her nose after a day in the cannery. Best of all she watched the water and the ships from the door. Each day she drew the the whalers and merchants who embarked and disembarked the ships coming and going from the harbor. She struggled to get it right, but the drawings never meshed exactly with what she saw. She hated that she was unable render reality faithfully on her pad.

At first she thought the two men arguing outside the laundry were merchants, they were too well-dressed to be whalers and one of the men carried a large art pad, a big brother to her own. She looked back into the laundry and saw her mother was occupied; it looked as if she would be for a while. So, Raisa grabbed her pad and pencil and stepped outside.

She hoped to get a peek at the hidden art. Unfortunately, the man had wrapped a large twill ribbon around the pad, which meant that even the wind couldn't accidentally expose the inside to Raisa's hungry eyes. He was young with good bones and a patrician face and about the age of Raisa's fiancé before the Czar had come for him. She felt her chest tighten a bit at the memory, but she bent forward a bit to hear better.

"I paid you in advance," the older man said in a melodious voice that reminded Raisa of her father. He was speaking English, but it was strangely accented. "If you are not going to accompany us, you must return it."

"I told you, I don't have the money. When you return to New York I'll be able to pay you every penny."

"Too bad for you. You gave your word. I need an artist on this journey, so you have to come."

"I can't. I am to get married."

"The girl will wait."

"She'll wait forever if I die in the ice," the young man retorted.

"Is that what's up? You're afraid?" The older man spit into the snow. "Get your courage up. You're going or you'll find me a replacement artist." He stalked off.

The younger man sagged. Raisa felt sorry for him. She approached him, her own art pad held protectively in front of her.

"Excuse me," she said, concentrating on using her best English.

He looked down at her and stepped back a pace away. "I'm not interested," he said.

It's the fish gut smell, she thought. But she hurriedly closed the distance between them. She wouldn't have a better chance.

"I can help you," she said.

"I'm engaged. I, er, don't need that." He stepped back again, staring at her. She realized she probably looked pretty bad.

"I'm an artist, too," she said, holding out her pad to him. "I want to take your place as the artist on that ship."

He stopped and looked at her, clearly skeptical. "I can't give you the advance money he gave me."

"I know. I heard you tell him that. But maybe I can get something else."

"What?"

He looked suspicious, so Raisa continued quickly "My family and I need to get to New York. You said that ship was docking there. I can serve as an artist if my family can come, as well."

He shook his head. "It's a scientific expedition, not a passenger vessel. Besides it's too dangerous. They're headed into the Arctic."

"Please, just speak to the captain for me. This helps both of us."

"Let me see." He roughly took her art pad and flipped through the pages. Something caught his eye and he stopped and looked at her. "You drew this one?"

"I drew all of them," she said. She tried to keep the annoyance and chill from her voice, but she wasn't entirely successful. He didn't seem to notice.

"It's good work. Almost as good as a mans."

She didn't trust herself to respond to that.

"Okay, I'll talk to the captain for you. What is your offer?"

"I'll work for him in exchange for money and passage to New York for me, my parents, and my brother."

He smiled, and then he looked down at her and his smile faded. "I shouldn't do this. You're a sweet little thing. You may die."

She shrugged. "Better to die on an adventure than live surrounded by fish guts. Besides, my father needs to get to New York City."

He laughed and she thought his laugh went well with his patrician features. It was a good, melodious laugh. "My name is Samuel Wellstone. What's yours?"

"I am Raisa Newberger and I am delighted to meet you, sir." She proffered her hand as she had been taught long-ago in an etiquette class she'd taken to prepare for a wedding that would now never happen. Samuel looked down at her fish gut-smeared fingers and shook his head. She was suddenly embarrassed by the stinking slime covering her skin and she blushed hotly.

He simply bowed quickly to her and said, "Where can I find you, Miss Newberger?"

"At the cannery during the day or here in the evening," she said pointing to the laundry.

"I will be back in a flash. Wait for me at the laundry."

When he returned, he was followed by a stout man in a captain's uniform and the older man she'd seen Mr. Wellstone talking to earlier. The captain nodded at her father who sat next to her outside the laundry. He bent his head silently in return. He said nothing but his heavy black eyebrows spoke fiercely.

"Here, give me your art pad." Samuel said reaching for it. She let him take it from her hands and watched him flip through the pages showing each one to the two men. "See, what I mean?"

"Why do you have my daughter's art?" Her father pulled himself up to his full five feet five inches. He was not a tall man but when he stood and puffed himself up, he had a presence that demanded attention. "That is hers."

"It's okay, Papa. It's for a job," Raisa whispered urgently.

He raised his eyebrows, but he didn't press his case. He knew as well as she did that their family couldn't afford to be too choosy. Instead, he looked at the three men as they talked, ignoring him. He scowled fiercely as if trying to protect his small family with the excellent action of his eyebrows and forehead lines. The steam from the laundry and the sharp smell of the lye soap rose around her. Mama would surely appear, drawn by the commotion. Raisa had to get this settled before her mother arrived.

"Sir?"

The men turned to look at her and Raisa felt herself shrink back under their gaze, but she forced herself to meet their eyes. Mr. Wellstone winked at her and she let out the breath she didn't realize she was holding. "Mr. Wellstone has shown you my art. Has he told you that I would like to take his place?"

"Oh, yes, he has told us, child. What he didn't tell us was that you are a girl. I'm afraid we have both been conned."

"Please, just look at my sketches. I can do this."

The captain shook his head slowly in negation.

"Papa, tell him."

Ever the actor, her father emitted a lengthy, dramatic sigh before pulling himself up to his full height and speaking in a deep voice with just the barest edge of command. Raisa recognized it as the voice he used when playing Prospero in the troupe's performance of The Tempest last year. "My daughter..." He shook his head lightly as if he were shaking snow from his head and turned to the captain. "Take my daughter and with it our fortunes, Captain. Her courage and art will see you through. Then bring her safely back to us."

"I cannot guarantee her safety. We go to a forbidding place, filled with ice and danger."

"I am ready," Raisa said. "Besides, where else will you find a willing artist in time?"

Mr. Wellstone laughed again, and the sound was contagious, a delight. She envied his fiancé in that moment. "Captain Bowers, take her with you. You will not find better today."

Grudgingly, the captain agreed to allow Raisa's to prove herself to him. He told her to present herself at the ship in two hours, which was sooner than she'd expected. She agreed immediately to prevent a change of heart, hers or theirs.

The ship she found waiting at the dock was a converted whaling vessel like the one she'd arrived in Nova Scotia on. Her art-trained eyes detected a number of differences. The ship had been reinforced from bow to stern with seven feet of oak making the ship look thicker and heavier than a run of the mill whaler. Two smokestacks blackened near the top rose from the center. Sails flapped loudly on the three masts and the bowsprit. It was a majestic ship and she longed to sit on the dock and draw it. Would there be time?

She heard Captain Bowers' gruff voice come from behind her. "You're here. Fine. At least you have courage."

She turned and smiled. "I'm ready, sir."

"Let me make one thing clear. I am taking you only because the scientists insist that we need an artist. If you can provide adequate pictures of the phenomena they need, I'll transport you and your family from Nova Scotia to New York City. If you can't produce what they need, well..." He stroked his mustache and tilted his eyes toward the gray sky.

"What then?"

"Then you will be revealed as one of Wellstone's con jobs and I'll turn you in to the proper authorities. Back out now and I won't bring charges."

Raisa's face became hot and a staccato pulse sounded in her throat. "I am not a con. I showed you my art book."

"Wellstone could have drawn those for you."

Raisa struggled to control her voice, struggled to keep her temper. After all she'd done, he was going to refuse her? Because he thought girls couldn't draw? No. "They're mine. I can do this job. And when I do, you will pay me and take my family to New York City."

"I will take your family to New York City, but there is no money to pay you. We already paid Wellstone. Get the money from him when you return."

"But—"

"Or you can back out now. No charges. No problems."

"I'm not backing out." She would show him.

He nodded and presented his hand. She shook it. Apparently, the deal was done. "Is that your warmest coat?" he asked.

"Yes."

"When you get aboard, we'll get you outfitted with appropriate gear. Can you use a camera?"

The questions went on for quite a while. When the Captain Bowers walked off, the chief scientist, a man named Peterson continued the questioning. He examined her drawings, grunting as he did so. By evening, Raisa was given a large pile of flannel, wool, lambskin, and sealskin clothing designed for a man. She scarcely knew how to wear it all; it seemed overmuch. She fell in love with the reindeer sleeping bag, that was so soft and warm with the pelt turned to the inside. It was odd to wear a man's pants but also freeing in some ways. And they were far more practical than her skirts. The sealskin boots were much too large for her dainty feet, but a few extra pairs of wool socks remedied that, though her feet sweated within.

The camera was another story. Peterson showed her how to use it and then left it with her, saying that it was her responsibility to accompany any scientist who asked for a photographer / artist.

"Why use an artist if you have a camera?" she'd asked.

"Cameras are tricky in the Arctic and may not work right. Artists can show the color, which we also need. You have to choose which is best for each situation. We need everything we can possibly get. It costs a lot to make an expedition of this sort. We can't miss recording a single moment."

It took a while to get used to the routine on the ship, but it was definitely a routine, with long, slow days that Raisa used to draw, paint, and learn the camera. Everything depended on her art. If she didn't succeed her family would be poorer from the lack of her income. With no passage to New York City it will all have been for nothing. So, she practiced endlessly, perfecting the color, the emotional tone of the art, everything she could think of. It took longer, but the art was better.

She'd expected cleaner air as they made their way to the Arctic, but the ship frequently used the steam engine, which meant choking clouds of coal smoke would sometimes waft her way and the ever-present ash turned everything a bit gray and gritty.

One day, as she made her way to the captain's cabin to ask for candles and a bit of wine to celebrate Shabbat, she heard her name mentioned amidst an argument. She crouched, pulled out her pad, and started to draw as she listened.

She heard Peterson yell in a voice filled with anger, "Raisa's useless."

"She lied? She can't draw?" It was Captain Bowers, his even tone was a contrast to the near-shout of the other man.

"Oh, she can draw and paint just fine. She's a lady painter in every sense of the world. Everything has to be pretty; everything takes a year and a day."

Raisa clenched her jaw and her hand tightened on her pencil. What's wrong with pretty? Wasn't art supposed to be pretty?

"Is there a problem with pretty?" Captain Bowers asked, and Raisa was suddenly grateful to the gruff old man who hadn't said more than a few words to her since she come aboard the ship.

"She produces one, maybe two, pieces of art a day. That's it. And it's not all drawn to scale. Because it's Art with a capital A. Just useless."

Her ribs throbbed against the pounding of her heart. Useless. No. That couldn't be. Her art was good. Wasn't it?

"We don't have time to turn back. Work with her. See if you can explain it."

The door open with a bang and Raisa looked directly into Peterson's startled face. She tried to look as if she hadn't heard anything but they both knew it wasn't the case.

The following day Peterson gave her a crisp order to take more photographs, but she knew that if they had wanted photographs, they wouldn't have hired an artist. She needed to get faster, less pretty. She needed to produce more, and it needed to be better.

The next day she tried to produce more, but as hard as she tried it just didn't work. When she worked faster, the work was bad. When she tried to improve it, her corrections just ruined the drawing. She knew she should ask Peterson for details of what he expected, but she was afraid that if she did, she wouldn't be able to draw at all, so she kept drawing until her hands went numb. She shook them out, sending out a brief prayer to the Almighty. Please, if it is your will that my father gets to New York, help me draw. She tried again. Perhaps they were too far north for the Blessed One to notice her prayer.

Her hands and upper back ached each night when she rolled into her bunk, one of twenty built in pairs into the hold, with drawers under the lower bunk for clothing. She slept in the upper bunk because she was light and a girl. When she sat up, she could touch the thick felt that covered the wood. She was told that there was more between the ceiling and the deck above to keep out the frost and cold. It was the most luxurious travel accommodations she'd ever experienced.

The rest of the crew slept in the same room she did, except for Peterson and Captain Bowers, who had private quarters. The crew was friendly enough, treating her as if she were a younger sister. Her only complaint was the snoring. Coming from so many throats it felt as if it vibrated the very boards. Still, she adjusted to it faster than she thought she would.

After Peterson's complaints, she could barely look the men in the face. Did everyone know of her failures? It was a small group. People gossiped.

Each morning she headed to the galley with the men for breakfast, which was surprisingly good and plentiful. They breakfasted on oatmeal and sausages or bacon, dense biscuits and preserved fruit made an appearance every other day. She avoided the meats and judiciously chose not to ask about the fat used in the biscuits. If God wanted her to keep kosher aboard ship, he shouldn't make it impossible. She ate far better here than she had in Nova Scotia.

After the third day of trying and failing to get the drawings right, she retreated early to her bunk and buried her
head in her pillow, taking loud gasping breaths to keep
from crying. She had to get better. She had to. Why did
it have to be so hard?

Even with the blankets over her head she heard the bell
ring, calling everyone to the deck. She didn't think it
meant her. She was useless. Right? But it made no sense
to rebel and upset people. Things could always be worse.

As she emerged from the lower decks, Peterson grabbed
her hand and half-pulled her to the surface. "Where is
your notebook? The camera?

"On my bunk."

"Get them. Quickly!"

She hung from the ladder and dropped to the floor with
a thump. She grabbed her gear from the bed and headed
back up. When she was finally on the deck with the rest
of the crew, she could see why they wanted her.

In front of the ship there was a large ice arch big enough
for two or three ships which looked as if had captured the
aurora borealis. But it was the middle of the day, and the
aurora borealis only appeared at night. She dropped the
camera, which was seized by one of the other scientists,
and began sketching furiously.

Inside the swirl of mist and color, bits of lightning flashed. She tried to record the phenomena, losing herself as she focused on the strangeness of it. Was that singing she heard coming from the center? Never mind. Keep sketching.

She vaguely heard Peterson say, "Captain Bowers, can you bring us closer to the phenomena. We need to get measurements."

The ship maneuvered closer and now she could feel the lightning flashes, the tingle of ice crystals in the air, and she could clearly hear a strange soothing song, as if from a thousand celestial voices. Angels? In the Arctic?

In moving the ship to bring it closer so that the new phenomenon could be studied, the prow of the ship touched the edge of the mist and suddenly it engulfed them.

Swirling colors, strange mists, and sparks of electricity abraded her skin. Looking up, she saw all manner of people and ships from many places and times, as if all of time had been compressed into this very singular moment.

The singing voices solidified into one voice singing directly to her. Was that "Lecha Dodi," the song that traditionally heralded the start of Shabbat? When she focused in on the words or the notes, they fractured into another song.

"Welcome, Raisa," said an achingly sweet voice. "My daughter, you are very welcome here."

Raisa's heart slammed against her chest. Her stomach churned and the world became a dizzying cloud of light and sound. She could barely hold her pencil, but she continued to draw, as if the very day depended upon it, as if the ship required the pencil marks to continue its passage through the strange gateway.

When the mist finally cleared, the sea was changed. Where the water's surface had been clear with occasional ice floes, now it was mostly ice floes with an occasional bit of sea. The sky had darkened to dusk. Looking down, Raisa spotted a city below the ice. She sketched it as quickly as she could, but it disappeared under a stretch of fog, then reappeared again, allowing her to add to the sketch.

Everything seemed different than it had, but strangely familiar, as if she were looking at the world through a mirror. She sketched the ice and the coastline. She sketched the strange white bears, someone dressed in sashes.

"Captain, this is Thule. I've read about it," said one of the sailors.

Peterson growled, as fierce as one of the bears on the ice. "Thule is a legend, nothing more. We are a science expedition, not a chaser of legends."

The captain choked. "Where are we?"

"I'm having trouble getting our bearings, Captain," said the navigator.

The ship drifted into an ice floe and the impact shook the ship and everyone on it. Peterson dropped the camera and it skittered to the edge of the deck. Raisa was barely able to hold onto her notebook and pencil and continued sketching, single-minded and focused on her duty. She used everything she had learned to memorize and sketch the landscape and the creatures.

"Oh, my daughter you are an artist. Very nice. I can help." It was the silvery voice again. Raisa thought of the voice as Shabbat.

Her hands tingled though her body still ached with the effort. She drew faster. It was as if she, her art, and the landscape had become one. Drawing was no longer separate from her, something she merely did. It was who she was. The landscape that came to life under her fingers spoke through her.

Warmth radiated through her body, as if her fingers had kindled a fire and it was spreading through her veins. She felt like laughing, but she poured it all back through her fingers.

The ship continued to make its way through the ice choked passage. Mist floated across the ice floes surrounding the ship and retreated like graceful forest nymphs spreading their diaphanous cloaks across the ground. Everywhere Raisa looked she saw something incredible. Here a coastline sculpted in animal and human forms, shimmering with rainbows. There a pack of sea unicorns with long pointed horns cavorted in the waves. Her hands moved faster and faster across the page, but through some miracle, the drawings emerged whole and beautiful, though her hands cramped and hurt.

"Where are we?"

"Thule," came the same sure voice.

There was more mist and the ice closed around the ship again.

"Get us out of here before we have to use the explosive charges," Captain Bowers shouted.

"How? I can't get our bearings," the navigator said.

"Take us back through the ice arch."

"Where? I don't know where it is. None of this is on our charts. Our instruments won't work."

Raisa looked up, momentarily distracted from the beauty unfolding around her, suddenly aware that she was shivering in the extreme cold.

The ice arch was gone. We need a map. But how?

She flipped back through her drawings; there were so many. Page after page, drawn faster than she had ever drawn before and with more precision and beauty. Could she make a map from them?

"My daughter needs a map? Bend to your task. I need you alive for my mission and you cannot live here, right now."

Raisa found her fingers drawing a map, as if one lived behind her eyes just waiting for the moment to be produced through her cramped fingers. She pushed on, though the rest of her body, the parts unnecessary for drawing were cramped and pained. The map that emerged looked strange to Raisa's eyes, but exactly like the maps she'd seen spread out on the captain's table the day she'd overheard Peterson complaining about her.

"Go now," said the voice of Shabbat. "Go before the Blessed gateway ices up and closes. You will be trapped if you do not make haste."

In that moment, she saw a pale otherworldly figure of a beautiful woman, her hair as dark as Raisa's own. In her hands, glowing as if it were made of the aurora borealis, she saw the tree of life embroidered in the air as if it were the cover on the holy Torah.

Raisa stared at the majesty of Shabbat, resplendent against the ice. She suddenly wanted to apologize for not lighting the candles, for eating the biscuits without checking on the fat, for all of her sins against God and tradition.

Shabbat did not seem to care. She spread her warmth over Raisa and said, "Go daughter bring them the map. Leave before the portal closes. Do good in the world and I shall be with you."

She disappeared and the spell that transfixed Raisa broke. She gathered up her sketchbook and pencils. "Captain, I have a map and pictures of the landscape. We can use them to find our way back.

Peterson scoffed. "How is that possible? No one could draw that quickly. Certainly not you; not any girl. And what do you know of map-making? It's not art; it's science.

"Let's see, Raisa," said Captain Bowers.

Raisa handed her notebook to him, and the navigator bent over the captain's shoulder as they examined the drawings.

"It's good, sir. Really good." The navigator seized the book from the captain's hand. "I can use these to find our way back. Her drawings of the shore and ice artifacts are clear. We'll be able to navigate using them as reference points if we have to."

The captain smiled at her. "Good job, Raisa. Looks like you've earned your keep today."

She was warmed and filled with joy. A peace comes over the world when Shabbat spreads her cloak and Raisa felt it now. She hoped she could keep this feeling, but the world has many distractions. Who knew what would happen?

A month after arriving in New York City with her parents and younger brother, Raisa found herself in a large auditorium in Brooklyn. The invitation made out to to her and her family came from the Honorable Charles P. Daly, president of the American Geographical Society.

She sat on the stage, along with the scientists and the captain of the Fortitude, sinking into the plush comfort of the stage chairs, gazing across the sea of velvet seats filled with men in fitted jackets and straight brown pants. She stared into the crowd and looked for Mr. Wellstone, whose wedding had made her adventure possible, but she didn't see him amongst the men. The women in the audience wore stylish narrow skirts and bustles with colorful little jackets with rows and rows of buttons. A glittering chandelier that would have been at home in a Czar's palace swayed gently, spreading its light across the gilt-covered walls.

The mélange of voices sounded as distinct as the sounds of the sea. She let them wash over her as she imagined how she would draw the people here. She itched to grab her pad and pencil, but it wouldn't do.

She knew she wasn't as beautifully dressed as the women who filled the seats. But she was on stage, well away from close inspection. Her parents were both adept at preparing one for acting. They knew what would show and what wouldn't, and they'd helped her dress. She smiled at them.

Her mother had found her some clothing so that she could present herself well, but it was all borrowed and they fit her about as well as the gear she been issued on the ship. Still a few pins, some needle basting, and voilà she looked great, as long as she sat or stood very carefully to avoid ripping the dress. Captain Bowers handed her a mint and she popped it in her mouth, enjoying the fresh stinging taste.

"Ladies and gentlemen, honored guests," said the Charles Daly in a loud sonorous voice. "We are here to present to you wonders from the far north. You know about the Greely Expedition that met such a tragic end. And the Polaris. This is something even greater. What you will hear will curl your hair. What you will see, you will never forget. It is my pleasure to introduce to you Captain Bowers to reveal his adventures in Thule."

The captain stood and introduced the crew and Raisa. After that, the evening passed quickly. No one asked Raisa any questions, for which she was intensely grateful. She had no idea what had really happened that day when they passed through that strange gateway into the land of Shabbat, but she knew she would carry it with her for the rest of her life.

Her fingers hadn't stopped itching since they'd returned. She had to draw, to make manifest the world around her or go mad. She blessed God for the gift of her talent that brought her and her family to this wondrous city. As wondrous as the frozen land of Shabbat—or Thule as everyone else called it—had been, New York City was even more so.

It sparkled. It lived. It welcomed all of them.

EDDA - PYTHEUS' VOYAGE TO THULE

From the Terror Edda discovered in the sunken HMS Terror

Jörd

Each morning the same. Jörd stared
through columns of ice in Thule.
Madness! Howling loneliness and affliction.
Jörd's sorrow rang through her icy prison.

As large as the giantess was, her sorrow was larger.
She could not be consoled. Not by the ice witches.
Not by the cunning Kaneed-
ma with their furry wisdom.
Not even by the wind itself, as it repeated and magnified her lonely howls,
trying to console the lonesome goddess.

She could not be consoled, though
she stopped weeping.
Worn clear through, emptied of tears,
Jörd sang to the night sky.
Her song landed far to the south, in the iceless summer.

Pytheus of Massalia

Only Pytheus, beloved navigator of the southern people, heard Jörd's shivering refrain.
The melody of longing and adventure pierced his heart.
He swore to find her. He would cross
from iceless cliffs to icy fjord.
A stalwart mariner, Pytheus was radiant to
his gods, who loved him over all others.

Pytheus sacrificed half a herd of white goats to his
many-breasted goddess, Artemis of Massalia.
She did not answer.
He promised his southern goddess anything for her aid in the voyage north.
Still she did not respond.
So Pytheus took his ship, painted with two un-
blinking eyes on either side of its prow, and selected the bravest of his crew to accompany him.
They sailed beyond known lands and
across the high waves to Thule.

Jörd

Jörd heard him as he approached her prison wall
through the roiling, curdled seas around Thule.
She smelled summer wheat and riotous wine
and longed to taste the world in full again.
She sang louder, beckoning him.
Let him but open the gate, she thought.
Let him make the smallest portal. She would

burst through and devour the world,
so hungry was the giantess for the glowing hues of green and yellow and red.
So hungry for plants that flowered, fruited,
and fed the hungry, it maddened her.

Pytheus of Massalia

Pytheus heard Jörd, and this time her song was
not one of sorrow, but of deepest desire.
Ravens tore at his heart. He had to join the voice,
which spoke to him of fur-bundled nights,
curled against a warm woman adorned
with gold and tasting of honey.
He longed for Jörd's flowered breath on his
lips and her soft fingers touching his face.
He spilled grain into the sea, followed
by wine, both beloved by Artemis.
Then he drove his crew forward into the cooling water.

Artemis

This time, his summer goddess heard his plea
and lazily drew a portal into the land of Thule.
Let Pytheus see if he can take the land of Thule for me.
Then shall summer extend to the roof of the world.
Pytheus's ship sailed into ice-choked seas, meet-
ing not a fair maiden, but something else entire.

Jörd

Jörd saw the portal open, the wide
world at the gate, and she shifted.

No longer a beauteous woman,
filled with sweet promises.
Instead, white fur grew thick across her form, sharp
claws and teeth sprouted from paws and maw.
Hungry doom portended. She leapt, thirst-
ing for Pytheus's heart's blood.

Pytheus of Massalia

Pytheus of Massalia gazed in horror at the bale-
ful teeth, the mouth large as a ship's boat.
He ordered his vessel back through
the portal, but it was too late.
Jörd reached a paw through the gate.
The crew beat at the waves while Py-
theus drew his sword.
He stabbed at the maw of the monster.
But the waves beat them back, soak-
ing the deck, knocking his sword aside.
The frigid waters threatened to take
the ship to the bottom of the sea.

He struck again but his best sword
could not touch the goddess.
It was deflected by her fur. She
laughed at his puny attack.
Only gods can fight gods, Pytheus thought.

Desperate, Pytheus shouted for Artemis, offering
his life to his many-breasted southern goddess.
Offering all he was to her work: blood and bone.

He begged for her aid to save both ship and
crew as he sliced open his blessed left arm.
He caught his hot, bright blood in a cup and
flung it through the portal at Jörd's muzzle.

The goddess-blessed blood burned
Jörd's eyes like strong wine.
The giantess shrank from Py-
theus, wailing in bitter agony.

Artemis of Massalia

The goddess of Massalia, her brown
hair icing in the frigid air,
slammed shut the portal to Thule.
Artemis looked upon her work and smiled.
It was done. Jörd was contained. Thule safely closed.
Her new champion saved for future adventures.
She returned to the southern lands, satisfied. Powerful.

Jörd

Almost sealed.
A single sacred polar bear hair wedged into
the portal, keeping it from closing fully.
Today, when conditions tilt in just the
right way at just the right time,
ships sail into Thule on the solstice, navigating the bear's single hair.
Then the giantess reaches a single claw tip
through the portal to touch Midgard again.

THULISH FUN

THE GINGER
GAMBIT

CAROLYN IVY STEIN

Magnihild's ginger cat, Dagning, mewed from in front of the heavy wooden door, his soft vocalizations plaintive to her ears. Magnihild knew it for a trick and she wouldn't fall for it again.

Each time she opened the door for Dagning, the cat took one look at the snow-covered hills and the heavy globs of snow falling from the grey sky and strutted, his tail high in the air, to the kitchen. Once there he would yowl at the cook until she gave him an early dinner. He loved fermented shark stew, which, judging by the awful smell, was tonight's dinner. Yuck! The cat could have it.

Even with that, Dagning was the best of all possible cats. He was handsome, with pale gold fur gradually coloring to deep orange stripes thickly framing his face. Named for the dawn, he woke her each morning as the sun touched the sky by embedding his claws into her braid and swinging on it until the pain in her scalp woke her.

Arranged marriages could be difficult and, Jörd, Mother of Thor and Goddess of lightning, knew that Magnihild hadn't wanted to marry Caedmon, who was notorious for the lightning scars that covered him from head to toe. So the goddess forced the alliance in her own way, leaving Magnihild as scarred as Caedmon. But it was Freyja's love magic wrought through Dagning that created the emotional bond between King Caedmon and herself. A bond at once powerful and sensual.

Everywhere in Viking communities, when people sought Freyja's blessing on a union, they presented the new bride with a kitten. Someday, as King Caedmon's wife, Magnihild would do the same for another bride. But she doubted she could ever gift a cat as wonderful as Dagning. He'd been perfect, a friend and companion as well as a cat with Freyja's magic coursing through his veins. Plus, he was a great mouser, protecting the house from invaders.

Now he wound around her feet as she brought Caedmon the Hnefatafl set, a strategy game suitable for the cold winter days when they were unable to raid and trips to Thule were frustratingly out of reach until the Solstice opened the gates to Northern magic.

Today, the men looked restless from too much time in-
doors. Nights came earlier and stayed later each day. Men
who usually had room to spread out or the excitement of
a raiding expedition found themselves crowded around
long wooden tables carved with images of apples and
sinuous dragons playing Liar's Dice and betting more
than they'd acquired during the spring raids. Winter
amusements like singing and competitive storytelling
were fine in the evening but the long dreary afternoons
stretched from here to Valhalla with only the occasional
hunt to break up the boring stretches of time.

Õgmundr the Younger had inherited his father's ruinous
hunger for the dice. Magnihild hoped he hadn't done
anything foolish, but she knew he probably had.

Véfastr was a heavy man with a long white beard, squinty
brown eyes, and an ostentatious wardrobe of silks and
dyed embroidered wools. He sat down heavily near the
fire across from Caedmon. He looked ready to "provide
wise counsel," which meant it was time for Magnihild
to spring into action to save her husband from the old
blowhard.

"Caedmon! Shall we play?"

One of Caedmon's father's most trusted vassals and
now an advisor to Caedmon himself, Véfastr pulled the
Hnefatafl board from Magnihild's grasp and set up the
board. Hnefatafl board were usually made up of simple

wooden disks played on an alternating pattern of colored squares. This set, a special gift, featured tiny, elegantly painted figures depicting scenes from summer. The artisan had used a special technique that showcased the brilliant colors of the paint.

Véfastr pulled at his beard and gazed at her speculatively. "Have you given up on more suitable pursuits, dearest Maggie?"

Her face burned at the hated nickname, but she struggled to control herself. He treated her like a child to get her to act like a child. He wanted to control Caedmon and everything else. She bent down and picked up Dagning, burying her face in his golden fur. He purred, then climbed up on her shoulder as if he were still a tiny kitten. Finally, Magnihild trusted herself to speak. "Not at all, Véfastr. This is a game for true Vikings, after all; those who can still participate in raids."

Véfastr flicked his fingers toward Dagning with a light, dismissive gesture. "Even cats conduct raids. What they don't know is strategy. Hnefatafl is a game of strategy and ruthless efficiency. It's not needlework."

Magnihild looked at her husband. His face was carefully bland underneath the feathery scars that covered his skin. He smiled at her, as sly as Dagning. So, he wanted to see how this came out, did he? She purred, her voice sweet and low. "Which side would you like Véfastr? Escort the king to safety or trap and destroy him?"

"This is why you do so badly at this game, Maggie. You fail to understand battle and cannot see strategy when it is in front of you. Skilled Hnefatafl players make the best battle commanders. I shall play against your husband; a man who has a basic understanding of strategy, but who needs to play more games against adept players. You are not useful here."

"I've led raids. I know what is involved. Hnefatafl cannot show the truth of battle. Courage and grit carry the day. Strategy has its place, but the heart of the fighter is all that matters in the end."

"Then you will not mind watching men play this game."

Magnhild bit her lip, hard. Hard enough to halt the red miasma of rage that was building inside her.

Caedmon stretched, a large smile playing across his face. When he spoke, his voice was quiet but carried across the great hall. "Enough, Véfastr. Stop tormenting Magnihild. No more cat and mouse."

Véfastr pulled at his beard and nodded with a great show of sagacity. "Ah, but who here is the cat?"

Dagning chose that moment to leap from her shoulder to the floor and then conduct battle with a piece of wood that had popped out of the fireplace earlier.

"Dagning, clearly," Magnihild said.

Caedmon reached up and slipped an arm around her waist, drawing her close for a moment. The lightning that forever linked them buzzed slightly within her veins as his arm encircled her. It was distracting, a reminder of past pain and at the same time a tickle of pleasure that she felt whenever he touched her, almost a residue of spent passion. She leaned against him, relaxing into the embrace.

"Sweetheart, I know you have gone on raids with your father, but Véfastr is right. We cannot fight our way out of a losing strategy. Strategy comes first." As he spoke, he selected the pieces representing the side escorting the King to safety and set them up on his squares.

Magnihild pulled away. "Bold action beats strategy every time. Commanders too safe and measured bring more ships to defeat than anything else."

Véfastr snorted. "Some problems can be solved by a quick and brutal demonstration of force. Most of the time, negotiation is superior and strategic thinking beats all, as your husband knows when he listens to the wisdom of elders."

"Don't get any ideas, Véfastr," Magnihild said. "King Caedmon is protected by an elite force and if you somehow manage to get past it, you will deal with me."

A smile creased the old man's face. "Never would I wish to face Magnihild the Lightning Scarred in battle, Majesty. No, this battle is purely fantastical. It is an opportunity to give Caedmon a chance to see how difficult it can be for his vassals to defend him and to persuade him to be wiser in his strategic choices."

"Less talk, more play," Caedmon grunted, but a smile broke across his face as well.

Dagning mewed softly, brushing against Magnihild's wool-clad ankles, little sparks of lightning tickled the air. Sparks shivered through the scars across Magnihild's body and it felt, in a small way, as if the goddess Jörd spoke through her for that barest moment. But there was nothing here the gods wanted on this frigid day. The ships couldn't be taken out into the curdled sea until it was well past the winter solstice and into spring. Thule was closed to Caedmon and Magnihild for now, which meant Jörd was as well.

Dagning mewed again, rising up on his back legs and resting his front legs on the bench where Caedmon sat. He gave the table a speculative look and rocked for a moment, as if he were judging the distance between his paws and the board. A vision of scattered pieces clattering to the floor and a ruined game blamed on Magnihild flashed through her mind.

She reached down and pulled the small, light cat into her arms. A giant ball of fluff, Dagning looked much larger than he was. When he puffed his fur out and stood in stiff-legged challenge to other cats, he looked formidable. It was a daring display that Magnihild thoroughly approved of. However, Dagning's bones were small and delicate and his muscles lean and stretchy, the kind designed for leaping onto tables and disrupting boardgames, not fighting other cats.

By contrast, Uffi, Caedmon's ship's cat, was a rugged creature with dark fur, heavy muscles, and large bones. Where Dagning walked delicately, Uffi made heavy steps that were strangely audible for a cat. And was he as courageous or as loyal as Dagning? Magnihild doubted it.

"Your piece is mine," Véfastr said. "As you can see the job of the defender requires as much clever courage as the attacker, Caedmon. Watch closely."

Caedmon leaned over the board and pursed his lips. Then a slow whistle escaped. "I believe I see that you have walked into my trap. Perhaps my best advisor should advise himself."

Magnihild laughed at Véfastr's consternation. He looked down and brushed ginger cat hair from his fine robe, ignoring her.

Dagning twisted in her arms, so she loosened her grip and removed her hands. That was apparently what he wanted because he immediately climbed onto her shoulder and settled between her neck and braid. He started a rhythmic purring. It was an almost hypnotic pleasure for Magnihild, and he slowly kneaded his paws into her chest. On days when the lightning scars brought headaches and pain, she could be soothed by the small cat's rhythmic purr alone. Well, that and the potions the healer brewed, but Dagning was better than potions, and cuter.

The room was cold everywhere except directly in front of the fire, which was blazing. Thankfully, Magnihild's woolen dress kept her warm. But even dressed in heavy clothes she crept closer to the fire. Dagning was usually content to sit in Magnihild's lap with the dual warmth of contact from her and the glow of the flames, but with no more warning than a sharp painful claw digging briefly into her chest, Dagning dropped from Magnihild's shoulder, landed on her lap, and leapt onto the table. He crouched before the Hnefatafl board and yowled as if the game were a cat challenging his territory.

Caedmon, pitching his voice even louder than the cat's yowling war cry, said, "Magnihild, take that thrice damned cat before he—"

Dagning sprang on the board before Caedmon could finish or Véfastr could interpose his body, scattering the pieces to the table and floor, then chasing them as they dropped clattering to the ground. The next action was a strange song and dance as the cat appeared to speak to each piece, lecturing in a yowling tone before batting it into the corner, underneath a chest.

After the initial shock, Magnihild started to laugh. Then seeing her husband's red, angry face, she tried to suppress it. No luck there.

Caedmon glared at her, sighed, and picked up the pieces nearest him. Véfastr did the same. "Get that crazy cat out of here, Magnihild."

"Come, sweetie, come, pretty Dagning. We all admire your skill as a raider," said Magnihild in her most beseeching voice.

"Hah!" Caedmon said crossly.

Magnihild gave Caedmon an exasperated look. "Come now, my brave warrior cat, bring us back the pieces."

She crept closer to the cat, but when she was almost close enough to touch him, Dagning ran up the length of the hall and then back down at top speed. He jumped onto the table again and knocked over Véfastr's cup of mead provoking an outcry as the precious mead spread across the floor.

Finally, Dagning slid under the chest in the corner. Magnihild heard the click-clack of the wooden Hnefatafl pieces banging against each other. It sounded as if there were a lot of them. Was it all of them? Couldn't be. Caedmon had some in his hand. But the rest? She didn't want to crawl around on the dirty floor darkening her best everyday dress. But even worse would be someone else touching her cat, so she knelt near him.

"Sweet Dagning," she said, cooing at the cat, who looked unimpressed by her blandishments. "Would you like a treat?"

She pointed at the slender boy hovering near the game, shifting from foot to foot. "Kætill, bring me some of the leftover club fish. Tell Cook that it is for Dagning. And bring a girl to clean up the spilled mead for Véfastr."

He nodded and moved quickly to the kitchen.

"We have less than half the pieces left," Caedmon said. He said each word with slow emphasis, as if he were talking to a recalcitrant servant. "That set was brought as a peace gift from the king of the Polska. It is irreplaceable. We must find the pieces."

"I am trying, my beloved husband. We all know that you, our majesty, is known for his patience. A little patience here would help." She made an effort to keep the irritation from her voice, hoping that her own even temper would bring him back to his normal easy manner. He was the calm one and she the firebrand normally.

The winter must be getting to Caedmon, she thought.

The spot by the wall underneath the carved chest was warm. Not fire warm, but sunshine warm, which was odd. The sun was shining outside, but the world was cold. Usually the walls were the coldest parts of any room unless they were near the fireplace. This spot was as far from the fireplace as could be. Could the carved chest with its intertwining dragons be the source of the heat?

She knelt down to pet Dagning with one hand as she used the other to seek out the wooden pieces of the Hnefatafl game. Her strokes brought sparks from Dagning's fur. She shocked the cat and sparks flew along the tracks lacing Magnihild's body.

It almost felt like Jörd's powerful lightning, but this power was different, lighter and sweeter, and she thought she smelled apples and the warm textured breath of summer grasses mixed with the musk of animals.

Dagning slipped further under the chest until only his tail twitching back and forth could be seen. Magnihild knelt down and flattened onto her belly, trying to see what lay under the chest. She pushed her hands into the dark trying to ignore the dust that threatened to make her sneeze.

The floor felt dusty and hard below her probing fingers. She couldn't feel any of the game pieces. So many had been lost she was sure they'd been pushed under the chest. If they were not here, where were they? She pushed her hands closer to the wall. It felt warmer and softer, like loamy ground instead of hard wood planks.

Dagning mewed, and with the sound came more sparks that temporarily brightened everything underneath the chest. Through a hole in the wall, Magnihild could see a field of grass and flowers, midsummer in all its glorious, verdant greenery. The mead hall and the snowy world outside felt small in comparison to the world Magnihild glimpsed beyond the small, cat-sized portal.

She saw thousands of game pieces, all laid out neatly on a green field, and in front of each one a ginger paw pushed them forward.

Were all the world's cats playing their own game? If so, it was a game Magnihild couldn't quite figure out.

She pushed herself further under the chest until her rear hit a lower plank, making the entire chest rock slightly. Dagning's whiskers brushed her skin and sent prickles of lighting rippling along her arm. She shuddered, but she continued to press her hand into the green field, feeling her way toward the closest piece.

As she touched the small, colorful wooden disk painted with flowers another hand did as well. Then a small velvet paw. All three melded around the game piece and it wasn't lightning that flooded Magnihild's goddess-etched channels, as had happened when Jörd sent power through her, but the cool, vital, glacier water that melted each summer and refroze each winter.

Flowers smothered her until she couldn't breathe in anything but the wild madness of a short fierce summer's blossoms.

Desire slid along the lightning scars like tree sap rising in spring until Magnihild moaned with frustrated hunger, conscious of her husband's blood beating within his body from across the room.

So near. So far. So maddening.

A voice that smelled like apples and honey spoke through Magnihild's mind sweeter than anything she'd ever tasted. "I am so proud of you, my fine cat, born of my own sweet chariot steeds. You've won the day, bringing me the prize I sought. Soon you shall have your reward."

"What is this?" said a voice made from thunderbolts. It tingled against her like lightning that strikes close enough to raise the hairs on a warrior's arm but no so close that it touched the skin. But it wasn't inside her. It came from... Where? It sounded like Jörd. But how? "You know that Magnihild is mine."

Another voice purred inside her like a thousand kittens. Magnihild wanted to roll around in that sound, to feel it forever. "Certainly, but Dagning is mine. My delightful servant who has brought me my prey, this one hanging from his little paw like a very large mouse. You are a master of strategy, Dagning."

Dagning purred. For a moment their roles were reversed and Magnihild's heart beat like she were on the losing side of a battlefield. She trembled.

"You are training the cat to hunt humans?"

"No, of course not, what fun would that be? Anyone can hunt humans. No, I am teaching him to bring me those touched by gods."

"Why?" asked Jörd, echoing Magnihild's own unspoken thought.

Magnihild's heart felt as if it would burst from her chest any moment. Was this what a mouse felt like right be-fore—No. Don't think about that.

"Sweet Jörd, this is strictly catch-and-release. I'll send your human on her way with a sweet reward; no harm done. There is even a bit of good in it for her, as well as a reward for my delightful servant."

"Then release her now."

Moments later, Magnihild bumped her head against the wooden bottom of the chest. Both goddesses gone as if they'd never been. The game tokens that had been in Freyja's garden were now scattered under the chest. She gathered the pieces and placed them in her apron. She held it tightly to keep the apron wrapped around the pieces and to prevent any of them from disappearing again to Dagning's questing paws.

Sixty-five days later, in early summer, Dagning led Magnihild to the carved chest. Underneath, a small black and white cat had given birth to four golden kittens, each with a pattern that looked like Freyja's falcon on their heads. Dagning puffed up with pride and purred loudly.

Magnihild didn't need an Edda to know the meaning of this. For bringing her as prey to Freyja, the goddess gave him kittens. She looked down at the wriggling kittens, so helpless. Yet even now she could feel the power of the goddess pouring through them and she shuddered like a mouse cornered by six powerful cats.

Each kitten would have to go to a worthy bride. Thereby, Freyja spread her net wider across Midgard. Each goddess-touched gift was a piece on a vast Hnefatafl board that she moved and changed to further her strategic plans.

Who wins when gods play?

Edda - Burning Ice
From the Polina Manuscript

Six long ships, prows bloody, their decks filled
with death, Skarde Bjornekiller took his navy
through an ice ring in the summer sea.

Stinking of blood, they sailed through to Thule.
He chased his enemy, Geirleif Geirleifson.

But the seas shifted, the ice bunched
up. The seasons shifted.

Geirleif Geirleifson disappeared with his entire fleet.

Where summer once reigned, winter took command.

A contingent of ice witches met Skarde
Bjornekiller's ships as they made landfall.

One tall, lump of snow stepped forward, revealing her
icy visage to the sailors. The ice witch spoke and her
voice was like windborn ice scraping against yew trees.

"Who commands these ships? Who brings
these ships to violate our shore?"

Skarde Bjornekiller stood against these fearsome
women, holding in his guts with one hand as they
tried to slip out. Lifting sword in salute with the other
arm he said, "I am Skarde Bjornekiller. We come from
Hlesey and we chase our enemy to these shores."

The ice witches threw spears made from ice and
two of Skarde's men died at once their blood
freezing as it flowed freely over the icicle.

*[This section of this edda frag-
ment is too damaged to read]*

And then did brave Sigmund turn about, bar-
ing his buttocks to the ungentle ladies.

He grunted once, twice, thrice, and on that signal Frekason brought the torch close.

Sigmund farted a mighty blast that caught the flame.
The smelly fart shot like Greek fire across
the bow incinerating all in its path.

And thus were the icy hearts of the
Thulish witches melted.

BEYOND HUMANITY

DEEP COMPASSION

CAROLYN IVY STEIN

Yrsa's hollow belly roared. That, even more than the slight warming of the air and the drops of liquid water on her lush white fur told her it was spring. She allowed bluish light to seep past her lashes for a long time before she opened her eyes to the dim sunlight illuminating the interior walls of her bedroom in the ice-carved house. She felt her ribs, so much more prominent now. She'd grown too thin this winter. Fortunately, she hadn't mated this year.

Last summer, between herding seals and training young Kaneedma females to take their positions as seal herders, she'd supervised a group of Kaneedma and human artisans. She watched with delight as they transformed ice into more than a home for her and her cubs.

By the time they finished, the icy walls were a work of art with intricate carvings of battles and daily Kaneedma life. When the sun struck the wall of the largest chamber just right, the carved Kaneedma warriors seemed to move in battle. She wondered how the artisan had made that happen. It was like magic to Yrsa.

In her sleeping chamber, a three-dimensional carving of one-year-old cubs rolling around in a mock battle at the foot of her sleeping roll made her smile whenever she saw it. Aleutian artisans imported from Midgard had decorated the inside of her sanctum with seal pelt tapestries embroidered with delicate stitches. Clearly their small hands and fingers were goddess-designed for the work, unlike her large paws.

Time to get up.

She lumbered past a sealskin calendar with its beautiful Viking art surrounding a wheel depicting the two seasons of the year: winter and summer. This month was Einmánuður. The sadly underweight Viking trader she'd bought the art from told her the month polar bear cubs emerged from hibernation was called Einmánuður.

It pleased her that humans recognized the cultural dominion of Kaneedma people in their own minor practices, even as it troubled her that they called the Kaneedma "bears." It was a slur. The Kaneedma were no more bears than the humans were monkeys. She had the opportunity to make this point directly to the ambassadors of Thule from the human lands and they seemed to understand.

At least they promised they would communicate it to their people.

Their acquiescence to the emotional needs of the Kaneedma proved that Modir appeared to be correct about the sentience of this non-Kaneedma species. Not everyone agreed, of course. And some who agreed in principle that humans were sentient still hunted them because they were delicious. But, overall, the campaign to spare their lives was proceeding nicely.

Still, she would gladly eat a human right now if one presented himself to her before she broke her winter fast.

Joking. Just joking.

She was not immune to the delicious smell, but her study of ethics prevented her from indulging in even the fattest, most luscious human meat.

Damn she was hungry. It was always this way after her winter hibernation.

Björn and Drifa, her plump, healthy cubs, were already awake and crashing around in the great room, searching for preserved seal. But she had hid it well in the first month of winter when they'd all settled in for the long sleep. The hungry cubs were too old to nurse these days but continued to stay with her since they were not yet ready to hunt, herd, or fight on their own. Björn in particular proved clumsy despite his bulky muscles and thick fur. The less said about the seal slide incident, the better. Becoming known as Brown Butt Björn did not bode well for his future.

Well, she had done what she could with him. Today they would begin the long trek to the coast where she would offer him to the venerable Hildingr for military training. She hoped the old warrior remembered his time mating with her so many years ago and looked kindly on Bjorn. A Hildingr-trained Kaneedma would bring glory to Bjorn's entire family. If he survived, it meant he would have his choice of mates once he was old enough to challenge the adults for his place.

Drifa had delicate of features with white fur that stuck out in an unruly mess, but was far more sophisticated than her littermate, Bjorn. She would serve her apprenticeship in seal herding for at least another winter before having her own cubs. The challenge would be keeping adult males away from her. Her already enticing scent told them she was an adult, ready for their wiles though her mind had not yet reached the point where she could nurse and teach another generation. Well, what else were mothers for if not to fight for their cubs?

Seal herding was an art, and while Yrsa had a certain level of talent, it was nothing compared to Nanna's facility with seals. Drifa would thrive under Nanna's attention as long as she kept her attention on the seals and away from any distractions.

Last summer, one of the human artisans had created a false door to hide the pantry from the cubs along with a fake pantry as a double fake. It looked like it had worked. The frozen seal meat was still fresh and still there. She pulled out enough for a hearty meal for the three of them. She didn't know whether they would find prey as they hunted their way down the coast, but it was important to eat enough to survive the cold weather, just in case.

Yrsa ate her fill. It was delicious; so juicy with ribbons of fat. She sighed happily as she finished her meal.

She called, "Drifa! Bjorn! Equip yourselves. We begin our trek after we break our fast."

The twins bounded into the main room. Drifa squealed with pleasure at seeing the seal portion on the wooden table. The wooden table looked out of place in Yrsa's house, but it was a luxury given her by an old lover and she wouldn't part with it. The seal fat and blood looked even more delicious on the table, so she supposed it was worth keeping, just for the aesthetic beauty of it.

Björn didn't waste words but began eating with a passion. He hoarded every bit so that his area stayed clean. Drifa, ever consumed by drama, made a mess, but also ate every bit. Good. They needed to eat just enough to be active but not so much that they wanted to nap. She would deliver them to their tutors with the raw intelligence that a slight hunger provided.

Their breath through the long dark winter had melted and frozen over and over again until the snow covering their spacious dwelling had solidified into a protective shell that disguised and protected the house from outsiders. Perfect for a cozy winter slumber. But now winter was over.

While the cubs ate, Yrsa chipped away at the interior ice of the disguised entrance, showering her white fur in a snowstorm of tiny ice shards. She could tell by the quality of light that it was safe to go outside again.

No one stayed out in Thule's biting temperatures other than seals too dumb to know better... and male Kaneedma. Not that Yrsa was saying that the males of the Kaneedma were dumb, but she thought it significant that only they and the Weddell seals spent their time above ground in the dark and cold of a Thulish winter.

Yrsa finally chipped away enough ice to open the door so they could exit their home. The cubs had finished their food and were chasing each other around the table.

"Bjorn! Drifa! It's time to go."

"Still hungry, Mom." Björn didn't quite whine, which showed he'd learned something since last spring, but the tone of his voice was distinctly inappropriate. She walked over and cuffed him hard so that he slid against the hard floor with a sloosh and bounced against the ice wall.

"Dress yourself. We leave. You will maintain a proper demeanor with Hildingr, understand?"

Björn sighed, but he stood up and went to the wardrobe where his clothing was stored. Drifa was already there, fingering the sashes and matching them to her belt and pouch.

"Make haste!" Yrsa said as she widened the doorway.

It took longer than it should have but the three finally started their trek to the coast.

Yrsa decided to drop off Björn first. The longer journey with Drifa would give Yrsa the chance to give a few last lessons to her daughter, increasing her chance of success. Björn was on his own; she knew nothing of military training.

Yrsa bounded onto the ice in front of them and listened carefully to the resulting thump. She sniffed, trying to catch a waft of scent ahead of them. Deep ice had a characteristic sound, while the shallow ice not only sounded different, but Yrsa could smell prey under the ice, if it were there.

This ice pack was solid and deep and had no smell of prey. She felt the ice tremble behind her. She turned to see Björn and Drifa bounding about excitedly.

Well, no harm done here. As they moved to thinner ice, they would need to be quieter, but she'd handle that then.

They continued traveling, Yrsa sniffing the ice as she went, calculating the depth of the snow, and moving on until she smelled a seal. No, wait. It was something she'd never smelled before.

She bounded onto the ice with her full weight, over and over again, until it cracked beneath her weight. She did it again and a hole finally emerged. She and Björn worked to widen it, looking for the prey within.

Bjorn, anxious to eat, plunged into the water.

Yrsa followed him to assist in case he found trouble, and rescue him if he couldn't extricate himself. But once in the water, she lost track of her cub. She dived but didn't see him.

Eventually, she saw a curved ice bow with opaque water seemingly suspended within the arc. That was unusual. Ice bows were common everywhere on the surface, but to see one in the water was rare. And there was no structure she'd seen below the water that had lightning shafts sparking within it.

Curiosity overcame her. She went through it, and as she did her ears rang as if someone was playing ice music inside her skull. Her fur tingled with electricity.

She must have blinked because suddenly everything changed. The water was warm, too warm, warmer than summer. Blood warm. She swam for the surface, keeping an eye out Björn and looking for the hole in the ice.

There was no ice, and despite the warmth, Yrsa shivered.

At first Yrsa thought she'd traveled into summer, because when she came up for air, there was no ice above her. When she poked her head up, all she saw was ocean, as if her icy home had never existed. But a true Arctic summer was filled with life, with flocks of birds and a rush of sea creatures. Instead she had traveled to a barren sea. Where was she? And how would she get back to Drifa and Björn with no land or ice as far as the eye could see? More importantly, she had to find land or ice for herself. She wasn't a seal. She couldn't swim for hours.

Nevertheless, she paddled steadily, seeking land, and searching for Björn or Drifa but finding neither. She dived again, feeling the strangely warm water flatten the fur against her skin.

Everything about this water looked different, from the way the light no longer played through the algae in rainbow prisms to the strange emptiness throughout. Even the water itself lacked the brine that helped buoy Yrsa as she swam.

Her heart pounded within her broad chest. If she couldn't find ice or land she would die at sea. Her cubs would die since they didn't know the way to their destinations. She had to find her way back to Thule.

She needed information. She dived again. She could stay down for the span of 60 breaths, no more. Then she would have to surface. This time while she was under the water, she heard a strange sound. It was strange, rhythmic, almost a roar. She paddled toward it. A bulky object, like one of the human boats, floated below the surface of the water and slid past.

She surfaced again for air.

She didn't know how many more dives she had in her. Her muscles were weak. She ached and her stomach wailed. She hadn't had enough to eat before setting out on the trek. She wanted to find an ice floe to rest on. She needed to find a seal or something else to eat. And where were Björn and Drifa?

The human ship was like none she'd seen before. First, it was completely enclosed, as if someone had copied the shape of a seal and made a sculpture from metal; little windows adorned the side. She pushed her tiring muscles to explore. Even if there was nothing interesting about it, perhaps she could climb on top and rest. An opening appeared in the ship and a human clad in a black, form-fitting outfit slid into the sea like a seal.

Like food. She could smell the fat inside the black casing, and it drove her near mad with hunger.

Yrsa looked longingly at the snack swimming toward her in the water. It would be so good to eat it. Modir said that humans were sentient and must be protected. But Modir wasn't swimming in strangely warm waters, aching and hungry.

Yrsa recited Modir's philosophical treatises to herself as the human approached, the strong blood singing to her empty stomach. She completed her recitation just as the human pulled alongside her.

She hadn't realized how hungry she was until potential prey presented itself in front of her. No, not prey. A sentient species as worthy of life as she was. He could be someone's cub.

Yrsa knew that in another moment she would lose control. That must not happen. She was not a beast. She was the apex of life on this planet. Kaneedma alone had true philosophy.

She dove and dove and dove, taking a perverse pleasure in the strain it caused her muscles and the slight pain in her chest. The fresh water above changed to the strong salty brine she was accustomed to.

Too far.

The scenery shifted as she descended. Shimmering schools of fish, a species she'd never seen before, offered a potential appetizer. Would they be worth attacking? They looked so small, barely enough, but Yrsa was so hungry. Further down, a shimmering hole in the water with coruscating rainbow light broke the blue water.

Her chest ached.

She needed to surface, but she suddenly wanted to see the hole in the sea. She'd never heard of such a thing. And above her the humans were still tempting snacks. No one should have to withstand that kind of temptation.

As she drew up to the hole, she could see that it was a thin sheet of fragile ice with colors moving through it. She pressed a furry paw to the cold surface and felt the peculiar rough smooth nature of ice. But how was it down here? Where no other ice prevailed?

She pressed a bit harder and the ice broke against her paw, shoving ice fragments painfully into her skin, like sharp baby Kaneedma teeth as they nursed. With one arm inside the hole, she could feel the temperature difference of the water. There had to be ice on the other side, it was so much colder than the water she was floating in. Perhaps Björn was there. She needed to find him… and find something to eat.

She couldn't smell underwater, but where there was ice, there were seals.

She pushed through and found herself in familiar territory. The schools of herring scattered at the site of her. A narwhal turned in her direction. She paddled upward to, desperate to draw a breath, but she was not quick enough. Her aching lungs couldn't bear another moment and she inhaled frigid water.

She sputtered.

Her only hope lay at the surface, so Yrsa continued to rise even though a ringing in her ears and dizziness threatened to overtake her. She needed air, but above her a solid expanse of ice stretched as far as she could see.

There was no hole at all. She wouldn't make it. Her chest would explode.

Suddenly, a majestic woman with seal brown skin and white hair, larger than Yrsa herself, swam up beside her. The alluring odor of walrus, seal, and gull meat wafted to Yrsa's nose. But how? She'd never smelled anything submerged before, but this scent was so strong, and so enticing.

The woman's dress rippled around her, white as Yrsa's fur, but with shot through with lightning flashes of color as if the dress contained a chaotic rainbow.

The world shook above her.

Again.

The ice cracked directly above Yrsa's head. She swam toward it.

The woman's form shifted and she became a large, white-furred Kaneedma, so intensely beautiful it hurt to look at her. Jarree. The goddess Jarree.

Yrsa couldn't look away from the Kaneedma goddess of spring, whose touch brought summer storms, whose kiss ended hibernation. At the same time, it hurt to look at her. Jarree seemed to radiate spring sunlight.

Jarree pressed her paw to the crack in the ice and it widened enough for Yrsa to push herself out of the water and fill her lungs with air. She almost cried, it felt so good.

"Mama! We found you! Mama!" It was Bjorn's excited voice. Drifa reached a paw down to help Yrsa. After a beat, Björn did as well. With the help of her cubs, Yrsa made it to the surface.

Björn was safe! That thought filled her. She'd found him.

She lay like a seal unable to move while her cubs nosed around her.

A globe of white overwhelmed her senses. The only disturbance in the white was the large furred compassionate face of Jarree. It was as if she and Jarree were the only creatures in existence in a moment that stretched backward and forward through eternity.

Jarree touched Yrsa's eyes. The touch burned with more pain than Yrsa had ever endured. Even near drowning hadn't been this bad. She moaned.

The goddess' voice boomed in Yrsa's head like the mighty crack of sea ice before a glacier calved. "You have seen the future, child. In that time, no Kaneedma survives. No Arctic seals. Not even the algae."

"Why?" Yrsa asked.

But the goddess continued as if she hadn't heard Yrsa's question. "You exhibited great wisdom and compassion. You are worthy to be one of my own. When the time comes, you shall rescue my people through your compassion and wit. You are my champion. Find the others."

The cloud that surrounded the goddess dissipated. Relief, desire, and hunger to know more warred within Yrsa and she sobbed.

"Mama?" A worried sounding Drifa curled alongside Yrsa offering her warmth to her mother, followed quickly by Bjorn. They warmed her until she was able to rise.

❀ ❀ ❀

On their way across the frozen landscape, navigating across cracks that formed suddenly, opening passages to the ocean, they found a fat seal. It was so slow and easy to catch that Yrsa was certain it was a gift from the goddess. She prayed her thanks to Jarree, and instructed the cubs to do so as well.

It was only the first miracle during the long trek with the cubs. The most important was Yrsa's newfound ability to anticipate Hildingr's concerns and swiftly counter them when she left Björn with him. Jarree spoke through her that day, opening her eyes with compassion and wisdom.

Nanna's seal encampment bustled with life. A large enclosure held at least thirty fat brown and white seals that lumbered along the ice. The specially bred seals smelled delicious sweet, juicy, and fat. Yrsa's mouth watered.

Nanna herself had barely aged in the last few years, her fur still gleamed white and her eyes remained clear. She nuzzled their noses in welcome.

There had never been any doubt that Drifa would be welcomed by Nanna at the seal farm, and so she was. What was less expected was the presence of two humans among the Kaneedma, a man and a woman. Perhaps they looked familiar, but perhaps not. Humans were hard to tell apart.

"What is this, Nanna?" Yrsa asked.

"They have been sent by our king to look for you."

"Why?"

The woman spoke. Her Kaneedma was accented with the horrid screech of the brown Kaneedma from the Baltics. "I know we speak badly," she said.

That was an understatement. Their Kaneedma was so bad, anyone they spoke to would be driven to eat them almost immediately. But Yrsa didn't say any of that, she merely nodded.

"We will teach you our languages, if you will teach better us yours."

"They are ambassadors from the human realm beyond the rainbow gate," Nanna said. "Our king sent for you to work with them."

"Why me?" Yrsa asked.

"You shall be our first ambassador to the humans."

The man answered, and his linguistic skills were even worse than the woman's. It caused Yrsa to wonder briefly if Modir was right about human sentience. "You talk us," he said. "We make things right."

That made no sense, but these people were clearly Goddess sent. Perhaps they were the ones Jarree told her to find. Or perhaps this was Jarree's way of preparing her to find the right ones.

Yrsa didn't want to go. She'd spent exactly one winter in her beautiful new home, most of that time herding rambunctious teenage Kaneedma, preventing them from destroying the place. But the truth was that she had no reason to say no and two adorable reasons to say yes. The king's favor would grease the way for Drifa and Björn in the future.

In the end, she accompanied the humans to the King of the Kaneedma's ice palace where a well-appointed room was offered to her. She agreed, but only until the winter. She wanted to hibernate in her own bedroom, with the ice cub sculpture at the foot of her bed. She would make do with a palace until then.

EDDA - A GIANT'S COMPANION
From the Edda of Caedmon as told to Narfi, son of Mani

Lightning flashed around Eirik the Strong, dancing against his wind-rough skin and fine iron sword, never touching either. Every hair on his body danced to the tune of the buzzing blue fire.

A mountain in the shape of a woman stepped forward.

Her eyes blazed like the center of a volcano. Her skin was the brown bark of a tree. She smelled like fresh harvested wheat. Each step was an earthquake. Her voice was the mother of thunder. "Eirik. Why have you come?"

"Jörd, the giantess," Eirik breathed.

Her eyes were hot like the legendary forge where Brokkr shaped Odin's spear, Gungnir. A single tear from the giantess would burn him like the lava within a volcano. Her rage seared from her eyes. He had to make her smile or burn in her fury.

He made his obeisance. "Jörd, Mother of Thor, Consort of Odin, Lightning Bringer, hear my plea. I come to you in my power ready to set my sword to your purpose. You take people."

"They are ours to take, as are the goats and the whales and the field mice. All earthly creatures belong to me, for without the Earth they are nothing. Have you come for my blessing? For healing? For the embrace of the Earth? Are you ready to admit I am the true earthly goddess?"

"They say that you build an army to fight Jörmungandr, the World Serpent. That you grant magic to those who serve you. Take me as your soldier."

"You wish to fight in Ragnarök with all the others?" The earth stopped shaking and he saw a sly smile break across her vast, lovely face.

"Yes, powerful lady, Consort of Odin."

Thunder clouds gathered overhead and the lava within her eyes began to flow down her brown face again. "I am Odin's wife."

Eirik's blood ran cold. He took a step back as if blown by her hot breath.

He rushed to explain, "But I thought Freyr was Odin's..."

"I am Odin's true wife; not Freyr."

The earth shook under his feet and his sword dropped from his hand as he tried to balance on the shifting land. He could see his distant ship tossed by the waves brought by Jörd's foot tapping impatiently on the ground.

"For those who wish to fight, they speak to my husband or my son. Odin's are the jarls who fall in battle, and Thor's are the thralls. Are you thrall or jarl, Eirik?" As she spoke a pack of four scrawny wolves, their fur jutting out every which way walked toward him, eyeing him hungrily.

He picked up his sword. "Thrall, Glorious Jörd."

"Why do you fight?"

One wolf slunk closer, its paws silent against the dirt.

"I fight for the glory of the gods. Please try me, Magnificent One. Send me your lightning. Take me as your champion. Watch!"

He swept his sword in a circle aiming for the wolf closest to him. When it hit the wolf's neck, the vibrations almost caused him to lose the sword again. How was it possible that such a miserable creature had so much strength? But Eirik had trained to fight the gods' battles.

He sliced his sword through the air again and the wolf's head went flying. A perfect demonstration of his value to a goddess gathering an army. He allowed himself a smile as he turned back to her and bowed modestly. "I am yours."

"No, you belong to my impetuous son, Thor. I am Jörd, lightning bringer, giantess. I tower above them all. I encompass them. I have no need for you or your rudeness."

Lightning flashed imprinting against his eyeballs in red and white jagged lines.

Pain exploded on his right side and spread to his left. He pitched over to the ground, his fingers no longer under his control.

Sparks played against his fallen sword, illuminating it, causing it to shimmer with rainbow lights as if it were part of the Bifrost, the burning rainbow bridge that links Asgard to Midgard.

Though his ears burned and buzzed and he felt life draining from him into the ground below, he heard her last words, "Mine are the explorers who live beyond their time, touching the land of Thule, splicing into the beyond where all lives are possible. Mine are those who tend the land. Who grow the crops. You reject Midgard for the Aesir. You have no honor, nor true compassion for the Earth in whose bed you lie. You do not belong to me."

Jörd retreated and where she stepped two small lakes appeared, but Eirik was past noticing. He didn't hear her say, "I pick my own champions."

WAR!

Escape Into Winter

CAROLYN IVY STEIN AND STEPHEN K. STEIN
It was summer's longest day, yet winter's darkness closed in on my heart. The North Sea, so calm and blue an hour ago turned gray with the speed of a spear thrust. Violent waves frothed over our stern and bow.

Hersir tied down the sail. The god of wind, Njǫror, laughed at Hersir's efforts blowing my second-in-command's iron gray hair into his face and rattling the horn at his belt. Always a cheerful man, Hersir approached the sea and the enemy with identical calmness and good spirits. He looked worried now and that fact alone chilled me more than the destruction of Aspedammen village or the enemy ships rowing toward us.

The salt sea lashed my face. I welcomed the pain as a sharp goad to my dull brain. Angry clouds swirled in the sky. If the foul weather brought lightning, perhaps I could save our squadron.

Hersir cursed under his breath. "In the name of all the gods…" But he bent to the task again. I joined him. Combining my muscles with his, we wrestled the heavy, wet sail to better catch the rising wind and lashed it securely. We didn't have long before the enemy arrived. I needed a new plan.

"Can you bring the goddess to your side, King Caedmon?" Hersig asked, hope pushing aside the worry in his eyes.

I laughed. "The goddess does not serve me. I serve her."

"But if we made a sacrifice…" His voice trailed off as he looked at the approaching roundships and longships with their sails up and oars churning the water.

My wife Magnihild prayed and sacrificed to Jörd, as if that would bring the goddess' love and favor to our kingdom. Obviously it wouldn't, but logic doesn't dissuade her. I was disappointed to see the same childish belief in the man that had been my father's designated second-in-command and who had trained me in combat and tactics as a child. "This is not Jörd's fight," I said as I helped him adjust the sail.

"Magnihild says Jörd loves you, surely she will not allow King Caedmon to fall if you call her."

I grunted, not wanting to engage in a theological discussion just then. I am not so god-blind I couldn't see what was going on. Jörd was building an army. This was the sole reason she drew scars across my body and Magnihild's. They served as channels for her lightning.

She loves us, her select champions, like I love my soldiers. Or perhaps in the same way I love Draken Björnen, my longship, with her fortunate figurehead of a bear hanging on the neck of a dragon. The Draken Björnen protects us all. But if ships have prayers, I do not hear them. So, it was with Jörd. Perhaps she cannot hear our prayers. Or if she does, we are mere vehicles for her power.

"But a goddess's love is a powerful thing," Hersir persisted.

"Jörd will rescue us only when it fits her higher purpose. Until then her heart remains as cold as Thule itself." I squeezed his shoulder, feeling the stout layers of wool and canvas underneath his leather and plate lamellar armor. It creaked as he moved. His young Irish wife had embroidered a serpent inside a series of interlocking knots on his woolen cloak. I hoped today's battle wouldn't mar her handywork.

"See them?" I pointed to the mix floating toward us with all the grace and speed of pigs running to slops. "We will have invaders soon enough. We need to prepare the men for what will come."

He wanted to continue the conversation, but instead nodded and moved rapidly to Draken Björnen's bow. His stride was graceful, as if he had been born on the waves, more natural on a ship than on shore.

"Do you have a plan, sir?" a sailor asked me as I walked past.

"Yes, of course. Be prepared. This may get worse before it gets better, but we will make it through."

I needed a plan. I needed to channel ice into my heart and find a way to turn our purpose into something that would benefit Jörd, attracting her to aid us. She would not come for our sake. Or even for the sake of the dead children of Aspedammen, so I needed to find another way to escape this trap alive.

Hersir walked toward me, accompanied by a group of men with spears.

"Sir, the enemy is closing to board." Otto pointed starboard where one of the enemy's longships paired with a round-ship was filled with men waving swords and spears. The wind shifted again, driving the ships toward us at speed.

I nodded to Otto and shouted, "Shieldmen to the helm. Protect Buri."

Buri, our helmsman, growled at the sky, his wrinkled face anxious. "Someone here has angered Njord and now the god stirs up the sea and wind against us." He gripped the steering oar more tightly. At my order two shield bearers joined him on either side, their axes and round wooden shields at the ready to protect him as he steered the boat.

"Wind and water are always unpredictable," I said, projecting more confidence than I felt. "Be prepared to change our heading on my orders."

Hersir caught up with me and continued the conversation. "Buri has a point. Each time the wind shifts it is to our detriment," Hersir said. "It's uncanny."

"The wind and sea were calm when the Curonians massacred Aspedammen, leaving not even a goat alive." I said. "They were calm when our squadron arrived."

Hersir shuddered; I understood. We'd arrived too late to prevent the slaughter. The scene we found haunted me, as well.

"The wind was calm when we sailed to punish the men who stained my land with blood," I continued. They were good odds, I'd thought: our eight ships against their ten. We'd pursued the murderous bastards into the sea, trusting skill to make up for the enemy's slight numerical advantage. Within half an hour, another fifteen enemy roundships, driven by a fresh wind and teeming with fighters, joined the battle.

Hersir was silent as we prepared the ship for battle. Finally, the words burst from him, as if he could no longer keep them back. "Why kill all the villagers? Why not spare the children or seize the healthy men and women as thralls? And why fight here at sea?"

I paused before saying simply, "They're not raiders."

That was the crux of it. These men weren't raiders, which meant their actions were senseless. Raiding was just that, you went in, killed when you had to, and stayed just long enough to grab the valuables. Then you left. There was no sense in fighting unnecessarily. No reason to kill every man, woman, child, and goat in a village.

"What are they?"

"I don't know."

As we watched, unable to interfere, the enemy cut our smallest ship from the security of the fleet like wolves picking out and circling a wounded caribou. They flung pots of burning pitch at the trapped ship. The wind picked up, fanned the flames and subsumed the screams of the ship's brave crew into the wild howls of gales. After they captured the second ship the wind fought on the side of the enemy, forcing back our ships.

Two more of our ships succumbed, and the enemy closed on us, pulling alongside with surprising ease. Thrown grappling hooks snagged Draken Björnen's rigging and a wooden boarding ramp clunked against the deck.

Heavy men stinking of spilt blood and garlic thundered across the ramp, axes still stained with the blood of Aspedammen's children, shouting garble in a southern tongue.

With guttural shouts, my personal guard surrounded me, shields out, just as they'd practiced many times. Together we pushed forward against the men streaming from the ramp, attempting to knock them into the sea.

My ship rolled in the rough waves and then rolled back, pointing her dragon nose upward and then down again. Over and over again as the dark gray sea roiled, men filled the deck with a spreading pool of blood. Through it, Draken Björnen rocked like a live thing trying to throw off intruders.

I focused, and the battle slowed down. The ships surrounding us became more distinct. I could make out their rigging, the overlapped planking of their hull, the enemy's mail, and even a small bag of yellow cloth that seemed to glow in the meagre light. My heartbeat slowed and my mind cleared.

Draken Björnen crested another wave, better revealing the watery battlefield. Four longships remained of my squadron—the largest and most maneuverable, all with sails unfurled to catch the wind and augment their rowers.

The enemy maneuvered to surround us, eight wind-driven roundships from one direction, its six oar-driven longships from another. The roundships were refitted merchants but two were as large as Draken Björnen. Their warships were smaller but there were so many of them along with the roundships it was like gulls mobbing a hawk. Enough gulls and the hawk must flee.

Their strategy shouldn't be working. Using roundships and longships in this way could only work if the wind favored the fleet every single time.

A wave crashed down and rolled across the deck, loosening my feet. I windmilled my arms, fought to stay upright, failed, and crashed into my shieldmen. A strong arm steadied me as I stood. The sudden waves caught others, as well. Two would-be boarders crossing the wooden bridge were swept over the side. This one bit of luck filled me with fierce joy, but the wave also swept Thorbert from the ship. He'd been the first to take the fight to the enemy as they boarded. Others grabbed the ship's rail to steady themselves.

"Thorbert overboard," I called out. Two of my shieldmen ran to assist, hacking through one enemy soldier's leg to reach the starboard side where Thorbert had gone over.

The lead enemy ship scraped alongside Draken Björnen. It was faster than the rest and was maneuvered with more skill. More men boarded and the din of swords against swords, swords against wood, and axes against flesh abraded my ears. One of them, a slender, bare-chested, middle-aged man wearing blood-stained breeches, clutched a sword, wielding it with no more finesse than a thrall using a club. But even clubs are effective when you bring them down hard on another man's head, which he did, shattering the skull of one of my shieldbearers, splattering blood, brain, and bone in all directions.

I lunged, plunging my sword into the idiot's chest. He made no attempt to parry, and the blade sank deep. He crumpled, falling from my blade to reveal a ghastly, gore-field wound and added his blood to the rest spilled that day.

On the ship alongside us, the enemy commander raised his left hand. A brilliant yellow light shone from his fingers and the wind carried an aroma of warm bread past us. He twirled a cloth over his head, saying something I couldn't make out.

The winds picked up, howling like a spurned woman. Was he controlling the wind through his spells, through the cloth, or was it just coincidence? Another mystery to solve.

I raised my voice, keeping it even and calm. "Otto, your team protects the forecastle. No one who enters that space lives. Got it?"

Otto raised his sword and brought it down on the nearest bare-headed barbarian, cleaving it in two and laughed. "One down!" he said in answer. Otto was the right man in the right space. One of the most powerful fighters Draken Bjornen had and utterly fearless, he would organize the resistance against the filthy southern barbarians.

"Sir, it's the Knud Hrolf! She survived! Shall I signal her?" Raud asked, his youthful face suffused with hope. A bit of brightness on the edge of the water caught my eye. Was it…? Yes, the Knud Hrolf, the smallest ship in my squadron, one I'd thought lost. It was far away but approaching rapidly. My heart surged with joy. Perhaps the tide of battle had shifted. Or perhaps Jörd had come through in the way of all good commanders, by sending reinforcements.

I hesitated. Something didn't seem right, as if the air smelled of rotting death rippling with sour beer. After a moment I realized why. Despite the water soaking my clothes and hair, my mouth went dry.

They had filled Knud Hrolf with debris. Her heading would bring her across Draken Björnen's bow. If the thrice damned wind kept favoring them, a collision was inevitable. And if they lit her on fire...

I calculated the trajectories in my mind, changed their heading mentally and calculated again. Damn! There had to be another way.

The enemy's flagship, a sleek beauty of a ship with a fat, ugly gnome as the figurehead, moved to our starboard side, trying to herd us into the Knud Hrolf.

I searched the horizon until I spotted it: a perfect ring of ice just large enough for one ship to pass through at a time.

"Hersir! That's it! That's Jörd's blessing. Today is the summer solstice."

"What?

"It's the solstice. Jörd provides a way out for us. Use your horn to signal the ships to form in a line astern. We're going through that arch and into Thule."

Hersir swung violently at the man in front of him, his blade dancing through the discord of battle, chopping through the man's neck. "Thanks to Jörd!" he said.

"Row!" I shouted into the circling wind. Through the ice ring I saw the Knud Hrolf aflame, sailing into our path, or what would be our path if the ice ring were not a portal to Thule.

"What are we doing? We must turn aside." It was Riodr.

I gazed at Riodr, but addressed the entire crew, raising my voice slightly but remaining calm. "Men, do not fear death. The hour of our doom is set and only the gods know it. We cannot escape the gods or our fate, but we can escape these men. Rest oars, port; fast stroke: starboard. Through that ice ring."

The ship groaned as we made the tight turn. Ahead, the Knud Hrolf sailed toward us, fire licking the sky, scenting the air with the smell of burning wood.

"Push through. We will not burn today."

"True enough," said, Hersir. "We will freeze."

"Better to freeze than to burn, right old man?" I grinned, happy that Hersir had seen the same thing I saw. This would work. "Will our ships follow?" I asked Hersir, looking across the water as my fleet lined up stem to stern.

"They'll follow. They heard the horn and they trust you. They know you and the goddess will guide us through this."

The men rowed. This time the wind shifted to our benefit, speeding Draken Björnen toward the portal rapidly as if the wind were driving us into Thule or into the fiery Knud Hrolf. Could it be the god of wind didn't know Thule was on the other side? Or perhaps Jörd's silver paws were pulling us through.

Knud Hrolf shifted in the wind and suddenly the small ship's path changed slightly, but it was just enough. The enemy's gnome flagship was still sidled up against our starboard side, trying to herd us into the Knud Hrolf.

"Watch out!" Hersir shouted. He picked up an oar and thrust it at the enemy's flagship.

I turned to my shieldman. "Assist Hersir! Push that ship aside. We must enter the ice ring clean." They hesitated. I shouted, "By Odin! Now!"

The men at the stern unhitched their oars and pushed against the gnome ship's hull, slowly turning it aside. Again, I saw a brief gleam of yellow light. A final shove sent it toward the hardened ice of the portal.

"No. It can't hit—"

The gnome ship crashed into the ice ring just as Draken Björnen's stern pushed into Thule. The sea beyond the ice ring was lit by perpetual twilight and the sea was jammed with ice. Colored lightning flashed around both ships. From my position I saw the ice ring transform into the mouth of an enormous ice beast, with glittering teeth and a gullet large enough to swallow a flotilla of ships.

"Grab something, men! Stabilize yourselves," I shouted just before the ship rocked violently from stem to stern and back again, smashing the rail into my ribs.

Hersir sounded the order to brace for bad weather on his horn. I hoped the crews on the ships behind us heard and obeyed.

The ice beast opened its maw further and I felt a wind suck at the ship, crew, and aspiring boarders alike, pulling us toward the giant throat. For a moment brilliant light illuminated Thule. I swallowed the scream that wanted to boil from my lips as intense pain coursed through my entire body. Wherever the lightning scars incised my skin, the pain burned through.

The strange light didn't come from anywhere I could see, but it showed me Thule and an underwater city perfectly. Iridescent buildings rose from the sea floor covered by a shimmering dome, looking as if they'd been carved by expert craftsmen.

Then I realized I was the source of the light. The lightning flashing through and out of me was the reason we could see the city. For a blazing moment I was Jörd's light and I could see every inch of Thule as if seen through her eyes.

Then I fell into blackness.

I woke, and the world was dark, cold, and eerily quiet. The air smelled of winter ice. Everyone on the ship had collapsed where they stood and were still unconscious. It looked like all of my crew had hung on and made it through. A few of the boarders came with us, as well.

I didn't know how long I'd been unconscious, but I could still feel a buzzing through my veins and the crushing headache and nausea the lightning left behind. Good. Lightning rushing through me again was a sign of Jörd's favor.

I stood, checked the men around me, then moved toward the bow, checking the others as I passed. Alive, but unconscious.

I shook Buri awake. His face was greenish gray. He looked as bad as I felt. I helped him stand and led him to the steering oar, which he gripped so hard his knuckles went white. Or perhaps he was simply cold. We'd moved from summer heat to bitter cold.

A look of puzzled wonder lit Buri's face. "Sir, where are we? It shouldn't be this dark."

"We're in Thule. Time doesn't work the same here. I'm guessing it's autumn. Are you okay alone? I need you to keep us on course."

Buri nodded. Then shook his head. "I don't know where we are." He looked over the water and gasped. My gaze followed his to the sunken city, visible through the water. People moved within, but the water was too deep to make out details. The city's beauty held me like a glamour, but I couldn't stay to watch. We had to secure our ships before the enemy recovered.

Buri stared, and I shook him. "Buri, I need you to steer. Understand?"

"Yes, sir. Shouldn't someone keep an eye on the city?" There was longing in his voice, and I felt it, too. It was a great wonder, one worthy of exploration, but later.

"Wake up your shieldmen. One watches your back, one watches the city."

I walked the length of Draken Björnen, waking my men and instructing them to disarm the still unconscious enemy boarders and gather them in the bow. I posted two guards to prevent any mischief.

"Just toss them overboard," one man suggested.

"We are men, not monsters. We live to a code," I said.

Even with the sounds of the men rising, it didn't touch the silence. Thule's quiet was deeper than anywhere I've been, a primordial silence as must have existed when Midgard was new.

A rhythmic creak as the ship moved gently in the water sounded almost like the ship's own breath. The oars hung free in the oarlocks, tied there with twisted birch withings more durable than any hemp rope. The sound of the oars as they moved with the light current and knocked against the ship's sides seemed to provide a counterpoint to the creaking of the wood, the flapping of the sail, the susurrations of the water displaced by the bow. For a moment they were random sounds of the ship as they'd always existed, a symphony that spoke of home on the water. Then the sound shifted in my mind. The random noises weren't random anymore. The ship spoke.

No. It wasn't speaking. It was praying.

"Master of Lightning, Creator of ships, Ruler of men, Glorious Shipmaster Caedmon, I beseech you hear my prayer."

I stopped as still as a hunting crane, my heart beating rapidly. My ship, my precious Draken Björnen, could speak. Could pray. To me. I listened.

"We are in strange waters, Honored One. We thank you this day for smoothing our boards and scraping away the parasites that consume us. We beg you for fair winds and following seas. We beseech you, deliver us from the monster reaching its tentacles toward us, each as large as us. Please hear your ship's humble plea."

For a long moment all was silent while I contemplated what I'd just heard and the strangeness of ships capable of prayer. After a moment, the last of Draken Björnen's prayer penetrated my mind and my guts twisted. There was a monster coming.

I yelled to the crew. "Monsters below. Prepare to fight." I ran down the center of the ship heading to the stern while dodging spirals of rope, debris from the battle, and a few dead bodies. Hersir would still be near the forecastle.

I found Hersir managing the sail with Otto, looking pale but moving. Reassured Hersir was okay, I turned Otto. "A sea monster comes to attack our ships. We need every man at arms. Go, now. And don't kill the boarders. We may need them yet."

Even as I said it, I felt a strange sense of compression and something else. Fear? Sympathy? A vision sprang to my mind: the smallest enemy ship seen from underwater, a huge tentacle wrapped around it, now crushing its hull.

Draken Björnen spoke to the other ships. "Courage. Shipmaster Caedmon comes to our aid. Hang on! Resist the monster." It was followed by the dreadful sound of wood screaming as a hull cracked under the strain.

Odin's Eye! We had only moments before its crew tumbled into the icy sea. If ice shock didn't kill them instantly they would drown in minutes.

"Hersir, take one man and the ship's boat." I pointed. "That ship is about to go under. Save everyone you can. And bring me their commander. I want to parley."

"This isn't wise, Caedmonkin," Hersir said, using the endearment from my boyhood. "The enemy will attempt to take over our ship if we rescue them. If they die, all the better for us."

I closed the distance until I could smell Hersir's foul breath and feel the pulse that beat irregularly in his throat. My jaw tensed and I lowered my voice, letting just a hint of steel remain. "I am your king, not your boy. You swore to obey my orders. Do as I say, do it now, and as your friend I will forget your momentary weakness. And bring me their captain. All our lives hinge on it."

Hersir opened his mouth but closed it and nodded instead. He signaled to Svein who was noted for his brutality and strength in fighting, to follow him. Vott, one of our best sailors, was close behind. This clearly wasn't over.

Ice and water erupted into the air as an enormous tentacle, sparkling blue in the dim light, wrapped around the smallest ship and squeezed. The ship broke up as if it were made of crunchy skonrogge bread.

My warriors collected around me, shields out, as I moved down the ship issuing orders. "Nock arrows and fire at the beast."

I hoped my fleet's other three ships were doing the same.

Across the waves, Hersir guided the ship's boat while Svein pulled men to safety. I couldn't tell if they had the enemy commander, but something glinted yellow in the boat.

I tried to sense the undersea world through Draken Björnen but couldn't. Perhaps it only worked while it prayed to me? Can the gods only see and hear our experiences if we prayed to them and caught their attention? Perhaps.

I prayed silently. Jörd, I come to you humbly and ask for your help defeating this creature, to preserve my life and the lives of my crew as well as these loyal ships.

I waited a moment for the familiar sensation of lightning moving through my skin and sinew, but nothing came. We were on our own.

A disturbance in the current near the stern caught my attention. I heard Buri scream and I ran toward him. I found him lying on the deck bleeding where a long, white spear made of elaborately carved bone had penetrated his belly. It was like nothing I'd ever seen. I knelt to check Buri, but I saw it was hopeless. He would die soon and there was nothing I could do about it except ensure that those who killed him followed him into the afterlife. I moved him to one side and covered him with my cloak.

A splash off the stern drew my attention. Two pale green men dressed in skin-hugging sealskin shirts and trousers treaded water. Each held identical spears and were preparing to throw them. A third's arm bled from what looked like an axe strike.

Archers near Buri's shieldmen took aim at the new enemy. The sea warriors sank beneath the waves.

"To me! We need reinforcements at the helm."

The small boat clunked against the hull. I saw about a dozen men in addition to Hersir and Svein. I let out a breath of relief. Hersir had brought the enemy commander as well.

I smiled at Hersir. "You've done well."

Hersir didn't acknowledge me but turned away and signaled to Svein to return to the boat to pick up more survivors.

"Commander," I said, "I am King Caedmon of the Northern people."

He spoke with a heavy accent that slithered like snakes hissing through his words. "I am Maksa." He held a small yellow bag which looked to be woven entirely of yellow light.

"Commander Maksa, fight on our side and once we leave Thule I will ensure you and your men return to your homeland."

He lifted a hand, as if to ask what other choice did he have. But when he spoke it was with dignity and calm. "I thank you for rescuing my crew. You acted quickly and I appreciate that."

I inclined my head, accepting his thanks.

"But the ice portal we sailed through broke into a thousand pieces. I do not see a way back. Do you?"

"I can return us home, but not if we are all dead. I need your help and the help of your men if we are to survive, and it must be under my command. Will you order your crew to follow me?"

He bit his lower lip considering. Finally, he said, "There is blood between my people and yours."

"I can see my way past it, if you help us here."

He laughed or choked; I wasn't sure which. "You'll look past our actions. That's rich."

"We can discuss that later. For now, I need an answer. Yes or no, Commander. I am out of time."

"Yes, of course. But this conversation isn't over."

I smiled. Something was going right at last. "Glad to hear it. Now let us join forces. We need to get closer to the monster. Can your men help row?"

"I can do better; I control the winds." His eyes gleamed as he pulled out the little pouch that glowed like a piece of the sun. This close, its sweet fragrance of wheat fields, crushed grapes, and fresh baked bread filled my nostrils with a sense of peaceful summer days.

He knelt by Buri and dragged the pouch through Buri's blood, which pooled around the spear still lodged in his stomach. Buri would die soon no matter what was done but it was gruesome to watch. Maksa lifted the pouch high and spoke.

A swirling cyclone made up of ice, sea water, and air appeared at Draken Björnen's bow launching water and particles of ice skyward creating a visible wall of wind and ice. Maksa exclaimed, "That wasn't supposed to happen."

I felt a deep vibration in the ship's hull and heard Draken Björnen cry out in my mind. A tentacle as large as two strong men squeezed the hull. Shattering strakes felt like bones breaking through my deep connection with Draken Björnen.

"Attack!" I shouted.

"Assist this ship's crew," Maksa ordered.

I glanced at the frost cyclone Maksa conjured. It was not that far from a normal storm. Perhaps Jörd would hear me now.

I called in a loud, clear voice, "Jörd, I remain your champion, but I must have your help if we are to survive. Give me your power so that I may save this ship and these men."

A silvery laugh hung on the wind, clearly audible above the wild winds and the scrape of frost on wood. I felt the goddess' gift fill my nightmares as the air crackled and hummed around me. Lightning exploded through my skin and sinews with a shocking suddenness. I knew the pain would come when I pulled Jörd's lightning through my body. It was agony. Always agony. No sane man wants to be a god's champion.

I mastered my pain and moved as close to the gunwale as I could, hoping the monster would reach toward me and make this easy. I held the lightning inside, storing it like a cistern stores water.

"Sir!" One of my shieldmen moved forward, his shield ready to protect me from whatever came from the waves. Others followed.

"No. Back away," I said, pushing my hand toward him and showing him the tendrils of lightning that wreathed my fists and cast a bluish glow over my features. "Defend the port side. Chase the creature to me."

A bone spear arced over my head aiming for Maksa. But before it reached its target, it caught in a shield with a loud thunk. One of my men's shields saved Maksa's life.

More of the sea warriors emerged from the waves and attempted to climb over our hull where they met Riordr's axe, which moved in a slanting motion and took off the head of a man from the underwater city. As soon as the man fell into the waves another sea warrior replaced him.

I needed to attract the monster to me before it crushed the hull. The ship rolled slightly. I sent a mental order to Draken Björnen to roll starboard, but either the monster was holding the hull too tightly to allow much movement or the ship could no longer hear me. Our new enemy threw more spears from the water. One grazed the Maksa's head, almost knocking him off his feet and left a trickle of blood on his skull. He rubbed his head and cursed.

If we had been in warmer waters I would drop into the water and bring the lightning directly to the monster. Here, the icy water might kill me. Would it even work? And what about the cyclone?

"Commander Maksa, send your cyclone against the ship's port side."

He didn't respond, merely held his little bag in the air and bit his lip. Soon, the cyclone pushed closer toward us. A tentacle as thick as the body of a seal reached up our starboard side and quested blindly along the deck, brushing one man overboard. I was dimly aware of Otto giving orders to save him.

I heard the faint prayers of Draken Björnen. It was enough. I fell into deep communion with the ship, the sea, and the lightning that filled me.

Now.

I wrapped my arms around the tentacle and released the pent-up lightning in a rush. As soon as my body touched the creature all the tentacles stiffened, displacing water as they rose from the waves. Then all the tentacles relaxed.

The enormous body of the creature bobbed to the surface. It could not escape my embrace, and as the creature burned, its skin seared to mine. Its corpse subsided into the sea, pulling me off Draken Björnen into the icy water as I desperately tried to pull myself away from the creature. I fell into the waves, aware that the cold water could kill me in minutes. Sparks hit the waves and created a small bubble of warmth as the remaining energy dissipated, but the sea was immense, and I was small. The cold moved back in.

Strong, familiar hands lift me up onto the deck and I felt my skin tear as I was pulled away from the creature. I looked into Hersir's worried face. He checked my skin, which bled, but the wounds were shallow.

A bone spear grazed my cheek then hit Maksa's yellow pouch, still held high, bearing it into the waves. The men from the underwater city cheered then dived down into the waves and disappeared from view.

I heard a voice soft as snow and sharp as ice, say, "Caedmon, it is time for you to leave this place. I thank you for bringing me such a lovely trinket made from a piece of Sif's yellow cloak and Njord's tears."

I looked around but could not see Jörd, which was both a disappointment and a relief. Where the cyclone had been, a new ice ring had formed, thicker and wider than the previous one, and sparkled with a golden glow as if it too had been made from pieces of Sif's cloak.

"Go now, Caedmon. You and your ships cannot endure our winter."

❀ ❀ ❀

The journey back to Midgard took moments in real time, but weeks had passed while we were away.

The enemy fleet was long gone. A gentle breeze blew, and the sun shone as clearly as high summer. The sea swelled with boisterous seals, whales, and other creatures.

Our ships—mine and Maksa's sole survivor—needed repair. Our crews were exhausted. We sailed for Fljót but when we arrived, we found only destruction. As we disembarked from our ships at the village, we saw evidence of disaster again. Bodies of men, women, and children, as well as their livestock, were piled neatly, as if preparing provisions for the winter. My pulse pounded in my ears and a curtain of red rage lowered over my vision. I clenched jaw tightly.

It was a moment before I found my voice, and when I did it was all I could do to control it. I turned to Maksa, whose face had gone gray. He looked at me and took an involuntary step back. I spoke carefully, but there was poison in my voice. Men who did things like this were worse than monsters. "Explain," I said.

He gulped and looked around at the evidence of death everywhere. "This is what your forces did to our village. Exactly like this. You think we did this? We were with you in Thule.'

"We did nothing of the kind." I approached him until I could see the sweat rising on his forehead and smell his fear. "This has to be your forces."

He shook his head. "Not here. We don't act without provocation. You did this to us. That is why we made an example of your village."

"Sir?" Raud pointed toward the brush. I glanced over but I didn't see anything. "There's a man there, hiding."

I raised an eyebrow. "Oh? Is there indeed? Raud, Otto, bring that man to me." I turned back to Maksa. "Now we will learn the truth."

They found and brought the man forward. He was exhausted and shaking, blood covered his hands and stained his bright blue wool overtunic decorated with Curonian embroidery and made from fabric fine enough to signal his status as a merchant. He appeared uninjured, though. Perhaps he'd held someone who was bleeding, his matted dark hair was filled with leaves and sticks.

"Who are you and what happened here?" I asked.

Maksa repeated the question in the Curonian tongue.

"I am Piške. May I have something to drink? I am too dry to speak."

I sent Otto to bring beer. Once the man had drunk his fill and stopped trembling, he told us of a fierce attack by armed, intelligent bears. They left behind items of value, but killed the villagers, scything them down like a professional hunting party.

"They butchered everyone. They ate—" He gulped and his face turned green. He buried his face in his hands.

Maksa said something quietly in Curonian. It must have been comforting because Piške nodded and continued.

"They took some with them, but left the rest, as if filling a larder with seal meat. I couldn't—I didn't—" He paused for a long time and then said simply, "No one survived."

Except him. What sort of coward was Piške to survive an attack that killed so many?

Maksa said, "That is exactly what we found in our village that was massacred."

"You butchered our village because you thought…" It was horrible, but it had a certain logic to it. Intelligent, weapon-toting bears storing humans to eat later. I'd thought only humans could enter or leave Thule and then only during the Solstices. This was a new wrinkle.

"Because we thought you had butchered ours." Maksa looked into my eyes and I saw he'd realized the same thing I had. We couldn't afford to be enemies.

"We have a mutual problem," I said.

"A pact then?"

I nodded. "A pact between your people and mine. Until such time that we can find a way into Thule and confront our mutual enemy or ensure Thule is closed forever to all who might seek to leave.

EDDA: PIŠKE THE CURONIAN AND THE BLOOD-SOAKED BEARS

Translated from Old Curonian. From the Kaup Longship Excavation

In the chilly hall filled with a trace of old smoke,
Where Gudrud's smile once
warmed the air, Piške wept.
Outside, white bears, their muz-
zles stinking of blood, growled.

"Stay, my Love, Stay with me here,"
Piške nuzzled his face in her hair.
Her cheeks once beauteous red, now
fading into ivory death.
Another body amongst so many
in her father's mead hall.

Her voice trembled, a forced gai-
ety, courageous to the last.
"Why do you visit me, Merchant? To
bring me trinkets from the South?"

"No gold adornment or teardrop jewel could
outshine your beauty," swore Piške
But her eyes, as blue as sky, were now as still and
cloudy as the pearls he'd brought her last.
"You outshine your jewelry, Lady. Even in death."

A battering at the hall door and two huge
white honey-stealers were through
Piške's heart froze solid, staring into the cunning eyes,

Not quite beast. Not quite man. But monsters that hungered like beasts,
and killed like men with spears and axes.
Gore-splattered human arms and legs
stuck out from one monster's sack.

Piške trembled and ducked down.
Who was he to take on the monsters, a
mere man before uncanny bears?
Unarmed.

Piške searched, but found not a single
axe blade on the bodies near him.
He looked wildly around but found
not so much as a fire poker.
All taken by the horrific man-bears in
their rapacious murder spree.

He knelt and whispered in his true love's hair,
"Gudrud, you alone were kind and good.

Now I rescue you to burn nobly in your funeral pyre.
Not end in the belly of a beast."

But how should he, an unarmed
man, stand against monsters?
Wits, not weapons, would serve him best.

"We wait, my love, for the dark shad-
ows of night to creep across the snow.
Then I shall hide you in the woods, my Gudrud."
Gudrud said not a word.

The monstrous bears kept coming. Some seat-
ed themselves at blood-spattered tables.
They guzzled leftover mead, making horrid sounds, roaring laughs.

A fat bear rendered a human arm, eat-
ing the meat and gnawing the bone.
Foul atrocities. Corpse-greedy bears.
They laughed and feasted on Gudrud's household.
Brave and cowardly alike were but
food to these monsters of evil.

Piške hunched down, barely daring to breathe.
If he could get to his pack, an amber amulet of concealment waited.

Piške pushed Gudrud under a stack of furs.
Let the bears think her part of the pile.

He crawled along the hard, wood floor, knees aching
Moving slowly around corpses,
Under the bear's noses
He inched along until he felt his leath-
er pack and reached inside.

Gripping the invisibility token, he spoke
the incantation under his breath
Adding a prayer as he did so.
"Blessed Veļu Māte, Goddess of the Dead! Your
faithful son begs you, Queen of the Afterlife,
Help me set Gudrud's soul to rest."

Into the chill of the hall appeared a goddess
with white, blonde hair reaching the floor,
Scented with daisies and white roses.
Veļu Māte slid through the insensible bears at the
solemn pace of the funerary cart bringing the dead.

Piske felt the burden of her presence driving him to the ground.
He bowed low, flattening himself, but peer-
ing up, unable to look away.

Her white wool cape trimmed in white
fur, touched the bears as she passed.
The growling monsters shivered and fell silent, gripping tight their mugs of mead
As if they knew death walked amongst them.

Veļu māte picked up a cup of the sweet
wine, took a sip, and cocked her head.
Piške held his breath.

She blew on the rim and fog appeared.
One death white finger stirred the mead,
Until honey wine, roses, and rot min-
gled with the smell of blood.
She sucked one more drop of the gold-
en elixir from her fingertip,
Winked at Piške, and vanished into the wisps of fog.

It was chilly in the hall, but death it-
self warmed Piške's blood.
His goddess bestowed upon him a weapon,
One suitable for a frail merchant.
Now he must deliver that mead to the bears.

He trembled to rise, but no bear noticed.
Invisible, he walked over bodies of former friends,
Of former rivals,
All silent in death.

His fingers touched the sanctified mead.
And froze like bare flesh on an icy sword
Aching, burning, freezing.

Then, as he watched, his fingers rotted from the tips.
And the sweet smell of death's per-
fume rose to meet him.

He shook, almost dropping the ensorceled amulet.
A drop of mead fell on one of the corpses.

Instantly the corpse rotted from the drop out,
Piške controlled his trembling hand.
So little time.
He dropped a bit into the first bear's mug.

The rot crept along his fingers.
He moaned as the bone deep rot
Ached like a putrid tooth,
And the bears turned their heads in his direction.

Not much time before the rot took this chance away.
No noise. He must bring the mead to each bear
But silent as death herself.

As rot consumed first fingers, then hand,
He delivered the potion to the bears,
Watched as they drank and fell un-
conscious to the ground,

Once the last bear fell into a long slumber,
Piške released the baneful cup at last,
His hand a mockery of meat and pustulence.
Aching, burning, rotting.

It was done. Now to bring Gudrud to her gods.
He touched the soft furs covering her
corpse with his rotted hand.

They deteriorated in moments.

He mustn't touch Gudrud. Not with that hand.
With feet and unrotted hand he rolled her body in a fur,
Then dragged her to the woods, far from the massacre.

He laid his fair Gudrud on a pyre and
consecrated her to her gods.
"Be at peace my one true love," he whis-
pered as he lit the flame,
Offering special blessings to Veļu
Māte, of the Curonians,
His generous goddess of death.

As the flame-flicked pyre drew Gudrud's soul up,
He felt her ghost's insubstantial kiss.

Veju Māte walked through the smoke
to touch his rotting hand,
Leaving clear smooth skin and glorious relief.

Then she caressed his heart.
He felt her rot spread throughout his chest,
Growing tendril by tendril.

She flattened her hand against his
breastbone once more.
It held the weight of all lives that had ever lived,
Their moaning and lamentations.
Their lost loves.

Each a sacrifice as great as his.
"Mine," Veļu māte said before van-
ishing into the smoke.

Dying inside, but living outwardly
The rot within him in abeyance for the
day Veļu Māte called him forth.
So it was that Piske sent Gudrud's soul to the gods
At the cost of his own.
The best trade he'd ever made.

AN ACADEMIC NOTE ON MAGIC IN THULE

by the Great and Honorable Professor Dr. Kondrát Boethius Beneit, Ph.D.

In my soon-to-be most esteemed work on the Eddaic Magical Theory Model (EMTM) I posit not that magic unequivocally exists, but that there is a possibility that it could have existed or may still exist somewhere.

Pause there.

Consider my genius. I know it is overwhelming. May I say, magical?

This is the key to understanding this book. Of course, more corroborating evidence must be found in a correlating location in space and time. Arguments over the Eddaic Magical Theory Model (EMTM) will surely focus on the texts presented in the slim volume currently in your hands. Think on the stories of Sif and Jörd, of Giants and Witches, of Thor and Loki, of Pytheus and Eirik, of Thule. Think and shudder.

The theories of Heliand and Drang Isle which I established in my last article (2018) prove my approach and the EMTM are sound. As everyone can see, the anima of the creature harnesses the belief of the corpus into reality. Obviously.

My discoveries of the Polina Manuscript and Edda of Caedmon further support EMTM theories binding impenetrable webs between my other theories involving the EMTM, as presented in 2017 (after the Terror's discovery) and 2019 (after the Vorcan's discovery) at the International Mythopoeic Translation Conferences.

The response to Ratramrus' letter by "the Opponent" on the topic of cynocephali, which I brought into the academic sphere in my 1989 thesis (Dog Headed Men Letter: A Response), has always been treated poorly by more conservative academics. Cryptozoologists and race-theory enthusiasts brought me on their podcasts to twist my words or chop up my statements. The foul Liberal media accused me of "opportunistic science" because of the melting ice in the Arctic. Is it my fault the ice is melting?

My incredible insights into Old Norse literature and archaeology and my translation abilities allow me to elaborate on how, when the EMTM is applied to the Polina Manuscript, this proves Feodor Curalis and Janiko Hwep of the Borlänge School are incorrect in their assertions.

Get that Janiko? Wrong, again!

The academic scholarship I bring together for this translation will change the way Old Norse literature is taught in classrooms for generations to come. As you read, you shall find that all your theories are missing a key element, which is essential for Old Norse scholarship going forward to function as scholarship, science via the EMTM. Soon all Old Norse scholars will consult my works before blundering into the morass of intricate tripwires found between translation and literary theory.

Scholars considered the Poetic and Prose Eddas to be the greatest collection of Old Norse literature for centuries. These stories have sparked the imaginations of annotational scholars, but the work translated here before you will cause them to Feuer Fangen.

As Smith and Sigurðsson (1976) stated, the "microcosmic embodiment parable in the perspective of macrocosmic warfare" found within the Eddas rhymes with that of the Homeric Greek literature, especially when using the EMTM. Such areas of investigation, EMTM, fundamentally uncharted, have established the components of the structural rationality of my analysis.

Thus, magic is real. As is obvious to all reading this.

Acknowledgements

Books seem like lonely projects but that is profoundly untrue. There are so many people who help, who motivate, or who do serious professional work to make books come to fruition. This is certainly a partial list because I have received a great deal of kindness as I've worked on these stories. I am deeply appreciative to the following:

Mia Kleve, my editor and one of the best editors in the fantasy/SF arena, amazed me with her encyclopedic knowledge. Obviously all mistakes are mine, but there would be a lot more without her red pen. You'll find her website at http://www.mrkdup.com.

Manon Chraszez Witherington, who takes as much joy in raiding stories for mistakes as Magnihild does on her Viking raids.

Jennifer Lopez of Mistress Editing who wielded her scary red pen on the first story in the collection. You can find her website at https://www.mistressediting.com

Konrad Bennett Hughes, whose expertise in all things Vikings was invaluable and who channeled the mad professor Kondrát Boethius Beneit to contribute his theories on Thule to this volume.

Courtney Luckhardt, whose knowledge of Vikings is as vast and impressive as her kindness.

Anthony Cournoyer who created the artwork for the Thule microsetting in the Micronomicon, a black and white version of which can be seen on the following page. You can find him and his artwork at https://www.instagram.com/sorrow_scavenger/

John D. Payne, who included us in the Micronomicon, accepted our microsetting on the magical land of Thule, read my Thulish short stories and eddas and provided critical advice that was much appreciated.

Thanks to those who read these stories and Eddas and offered invaluable critical advice including: Max Roprez, Eva Papier, Mela Eckenfels, and L.A. Selby, and The Boy Band (Ryan English, John D. Payne, Miles English, Nate Givens, and James R. Payne).

With much thanks for the discussion on naval tactics for the final story in this collection in which I learned a great deal, though mostly I learned that I had a lot more to learn: Justin Watson, Larry T. Davis, and David Cole.

Sandra Greenberg, for always believing in my writing.

For unrelenting encouragement, Astrid Harp and Helen Savore.

William Allen Webb for being a never-ending fountain of enthusiasm and advice on writing, marketing, and publishing.

Thank you to the tribe at Superstars Writing Seminars, who welcomed me in, taught me, and steadied me in the journey. And to my Memphis tribe of writers whose support I've relied upon as I stepped into this new world.

Finally, Stephen Stein could have fit in any of the categories below. He is everything to me. He is my best friend, best first reader, best historical and strategic source of knowledge, kindest encourager, harshest editor and proofreader, and so much more. So I'm just going to thank him again for being exactly who he is. I am so lucky to have him in my life.

About the Author

Carolyn Ivy Stein is a freelance writer. She writes historical, fantasy, and science fiction as well as non-fiction and gaming supplements. She has received six Honorable Mentions from the Writers of the Future contest.

When not writing she games and experiments with gourmet vegan cooking.

http://www.carolynivystein.com